MULTIPLES OF MURDER

Three cases for Philip Bryce

Peter Zander-Howell

Copyright © 2022 Peter Zander-Howell

All rights reserved

The characters and events portrayed in this book are fictitious. Any similarity to real persons, living or dead, is coincidental and not intended by the author.

No part of this book may be reproduced, or stored in a retrieval system, or transmitted in any form or by any means, electronic, mechanical, photocopying, recording, or otherwise, without express written permission of the publisher.

For Kelsey, Russ, and Caroline

PROLOGUE

Three cases for Philip Bryce.

The first two are set in 1949, and follow on from *The Bedroom Window Murder*, *The Courthouse Murder*, and *The Felixstowe Murder*.

The third is a 'prequel', going back to 1946, when Bryce – having returned to the police after army service – was a still a Detective Inspector, based in Whitechapel rather than Scotland Yard.

INTRODUCTION

1. DEATH IN AN OFFICE KITCHEN

In the office kitchen of a London advertising agency, a man falls to the floor, dead. Natural causes are presumed – until evidence emerges showing this cannot be the case. Chief Inspector Bryce is assigned to expose the murderer.

2. DEATH IN THE PUBLIC BATHS

A body is found in the public bathhouse in St Marylebone. Bryce is tasked with discovering the identities of the victim, and his assailant. With Sergeant Haig's help, the DCI sorts the facts from the lies.

3. DEATH ON A LONDON BUS

On the upper deck of a London bus, a man is found dead. All of the passengers claim they saw and heard nothing. Inspector Bryce, together with colleagues from Leman Street police station, solves one of his earlier cases.

PREFACE

DETECTIVE CHIEF INSPECTOR BRYCE

Philip Bryce is an unusual policeman. A Cambridge-educated barrister, he joined the Metropolitan Police in 1937 under Lord Trenchard's accelerated promotion scheme. After distinguished army service in WW2, by 1949 he has become Scotland Yard's youngest DCI.

Bryce's first fiancée was killed during a bombing raid in 1943. Just before the 'Office Kitchen' incident, he married Veronica, a war widow whom he met during an earlier case.

A very private individual, Bryce never talks of himself and has few close friendships. He is something of a polymath, with a remarkable fund of general knowledge – snippets of which he passes on to people around him.

CONTENTS

Title Page

Copyright

Dedication

Prologue

Introduction

Preface

DEATH IN AN OFFICE KITCHEN	1
DEATH IN THE PUBLIC BATHS	61
DEATH ON A LONDON BUS	159
Afterword	239
Books By This Author	243

DEATH IN AN OFFICE KITCHEN

PETER ZANDER-HOWELL

Tuesday 30th August 1949

In a kitchen attached to a large and bright advertising agency in London's Great Castle Street, a man suddenly stiffened, and fell to the floor. The four people working in the adjacent room heard nothing.

Some ten minutes later, Margaret Collins looked up from the corselette photographs she was trimming, and began to wonder where her elevenses had got to. After a further five minutes of adjusting pictures around the text for her lingerie advertisement, she voiced that thought:

"What on earth is John doing with the coffee?" she asked a little petulantly. "He's been gone for ages."

Neil Hazel looked up from his work. "He's probably burnt his toast again, and has had to start afresh. Our coffees are of secondary importance to him."

The two other men present in the office both joined in the speculation. Martin Lawn, balancing dangerously on the back legs of his chair said:

"I don't know whether John has any breakfast at home, but he certainly seems to look forward to his toast at 10:30 each morning – in fact I've heard him say he couldn't do without it."

The final member of the little team laughed.

"It's the fact that he has all those jars of marmalade that I find so odd," said Adrian Hunter. "A different marmalade for each weekday. I've vaguely wondered if he has two more for the weekend, but I've never been sufficiently interested to ask."

"It can't be that he's burnt the toast," said Margaret. "Haven't you seen his brand new Morphy-Richards toaster? He told me when he brought it in yesterday that it switches off automatically when the toast is ready – and you can alter the setting according to how brown you like it. It cost four guineas, apparently – I couldn't justify paying anything like that."

"Well, in that case he's probably just playing with his new toy, and has forgotten it's his day to make everyone's coffee," said Neil, losing no opportunity to take a swipe at John.

Adrian Hunter wasn't pleased to hear Neil's comment. Deliberately referencing a recent – and exceptional – failure for the firm, he delivered a calculated barb of his own:

"If that's the case, I vote we all give John another five minutes playtime, to show our appreciation for his winning the new Brewster contract for the firm. It's the successes like John's that help the firm survive a damaging flop."

Neil Hazel flushed. He didn't join in with the warm agreement from Martin and Margaret; both of whom he felt were enjoying his discomfort.

In less than two minutes, however, the quiet of the office was interrupted by an angry-sounding buzzer.

"Uh-oh! The Boss is also wondering where his coffee is," remarked Adrian.

Margaret rose quickly, tapped on a door close to her desk, and without waiting for a response went through to Julian Webb's office. She emerged again within seconds.

"Good guess, Adrian," she smiled at her colleague, as she passed his desk on her way to the kitchenette door on the far side of the office.

The three men had all turned back to their work when a noise – an agonised moaning – was heard in the kitchen. Before anyone could move, Margaret came back into the office, clutching the door jamb for support.

"John's lying on the floor. I think he's dead," she gasped, sagging to her knees and then onto the floor. She had not lost consciousness, her eyes were still open, but for the moment her legs had completely lost the capacity to support her.

Her colleagues reacted quickly. Adrian, technically the senior, bent over Margaret and patted her hand, gently telling her to stay where she was until she felt more recovered. Asking Martin to accompany him, both men stepped over the prone woman and went into the kitchen.

Inside, they found John as Margaret had described him. Martin, who had some basic first aid skills from his wartime service, knelt down and felt for a pulse. Looking back up he said in a shocked voice:

"He's gone, Adrian."

"Oh, Lord. All right, I'd better go and tell Mr Webb."

With Adrian gone, Martin looked around the room. The new toaster, all gleaming chrome, sat on one side of the sink. Two slices of toast protruded from the top. Martin touched them, and found that they – and the toaster itself – were practically cold.

On the table, six cups and saucers were set out, each already primed with instant coffee powder. The bottle of milk, delivered each day to the office, stood beside them. So John hadn't forgotten he was the 'coffee monitor' today, thought Martin.

The electric kettle stood on the draining board. The lid was off, and he could see it was full of water. Both ends of the flex were plugged in, but the kettle wasn't boiling.

Martin was contemplating this scene, when Julian Webb came in. Adrian followed, and stood just inside the doorway.

"Is he dead, Martin?" asked Webb.

"I'm afraid so, Mr Webb," replied Martin. "Has been for at last a quarter of an hour, I think.

The toast in the machine is already cold."

"God, him and his toast," said Webb uncharitably. "But John shouldn't be having a heart attack at his age. He can't be more than thirtyish, and always looked pretty fit."

"That's right, Mr Webb," replied Martin. "It's odd, and very sad. But I suppose they'll find he had something wrong with his ticker that nobody knew about."

"All right, Martin. I gather Neil has called for an ambulance, so there's nothing more we can do until it gets here. Not much more the ambulance boys can do, come to that. He wasn't married, or anything, as far as I recall?"

Adrian answered from the doorway. "No, not even 'or anything'. He told me once that he was almost engaged at the end of the war, but it fell through. Since then, I gather he'd occasionally asked a girl out, but there was never anyone special. When he first joined us, he lived south of the river somewhere, but a couple of years ago, when the Central Line opened as far as Leytonstone, he moved into digs there."

"Hmmm. I don't want to be disrespectful or anything, but I really don't see any reason why we can't have the coffee that he didn't get around to making."

"I'll do it Mr Webb," said Martin, who was nearest the kettle. "But I suspect the element has gone or the fuse has blown. It's plugged in but not working."

"Sort the fuse, if it's that, or ask Margaret to go out and buy a new kettle if necessary – she'll probably make a more sensible choice of a domestic item. Meantime, let's get back to work," said Webb.

Stepping carefully to avoid treading on the dead man's hand, Martin unplugged the kettle from the wall socket, and moved towards the inner hallway. This was a sizeable room which, like the kitchen, was windowless; the fuseboard was housed here, amongst coat hooks, stationery cupboards, and a general storage area.

"Does anyone fancy some cold toast?" he asked, as he passed the office doorway into the vestibule. "Or we could warm it up again, I suppose."

His colleagues shook their heads, Margaret in particular looking as though she might be sick.

Martin had a reasonable grasp of electrical circuits, and soon found that one of the rewireable fuses had blown. There was a card with spare fuse wire wrapped around it, albeit only 5 Amp rating. He renewed the fuse, noting that the remainder of the original wire was also 5 Amp.

As he returned to the kitchen, two ambulance men arrived. Leaving their stretcher in the office, they were shown the casualty. They knelt by the body, but rose again after only a few seconds.

"Unexplained death, guv," said one. We can't move him yet. You'll have to get a doctor first."

"I see," said Martin. "Right, we'll sort that. Will you stay?"

"Can't do that. More live patients to see," the man replied, and with that the pair left the kitchen, collected their unused stretcher, and went to help the quick.

Martin plugged the kettle into the wall socket again, and was about to return to the office to see about getting a doctor when Adrian returned to the kitchen, shutting the door behind him.

"Margaret's very upset, so I think we should avoid any more discussion in front of her.

"I anticipated the need for a doctor, Martin. I rang down to the porter and got the name of a local GP. By some miracle I've managed to contact him. He was about to start on his rounds but has agreed to call here first. When he has certified death, or whatever they have to do, we can get poor John removed.

"What happened to the coffee?" he continued.

"The fuse had blown. I've replaced it, and plugged the kettle in again but..." he looked at the appliance "...it should have started singing by now and isn't. I think the element has gone."

"I've had a horrible thought," said Adrian. "Is it a bit of a coincidence that John dies as the kettle fails?"

The two men looked at each other, the kettle, and then at the body by their feet.

"Are you thinking what I'm thinking?" asked Martin.

Without replying, Adrian moved to the sink. Taking great care not to touch the kettle, he carefully unplugged its flex from the wall.

"I'm thinking we'd better keep this to ourselves until the doctor gets here, and tell him," said Adrian slowly.

The kitchen door opened a crack. Margaret, avoiding looking at the floor where John lay, passed on the message that Mr Webb was questioning the lack of coffee.

"Sorry, Margaret, you'll have to tell him that the kettle doesn't work," said Adrian. "If he's still really chafing for coffee, I suggest you try Taylors next door, explain the position, and see if they'll let you borrow their kitchen this once. Mr Webb actually suggested that you are the best person to choose a new kettle, but perhaps you could do that later. We can't make coffee in here with John on the floor."

Margaret nodded and backed away from the door again.

Martin went back into the inner hall to check if the fuse had blown again, but found it was still intact. He returned to the kitchen to find Adrian still contemplating, and informed him.

A few seconds later, Neil opened the door to announce that the doctor had arrived. Neil, who had so far not come to the kitchen door, now peered nervously at the body for the first time before moving aside to allow the medic to pass.

A harassed-looking man in his fifties introduced himself:

"Good morning, I'm Doctor Atherton." Setting down his medical bag with a thud on the floor, he said, "Let's see what we have here. Just help me turn him over, please."

Martin assisted in this.

"Dear me, he is a young chap. Always a sorry sight," remarked the medic. A few moments later he stood up.

"Gentlemen," he said, "he isn't my patient, and I don't know why he has died. I can't possibly give a certificate."

The two men looked at each other; Adrian voiced their concerns:

"We don't know if this is relevant, Doctor, but John was in the process of making coffee when he died. It may of course be coincidence, but the electric kettle seems to have developed a fault and fused at the same time."

Doctor Atherton looked across at the kettle. He saw an old copper and brass appliance, and recognised it at once.

"That's an old one," he said. "My wife and I were given one exactly like that as a wedding present in 1924. I remember being told it was the first electric kettle where the water could surround the heating element, so it was supposed to be more efficient than ones with the element in a separate compartment."

He crouched on the floor again, and this time looked very carefully at each of John's hands.

"Hmm," he muttered. Rising again he went to look more closely at the kettle, and at the tap, but apparently failed to see anything of significance.

He looked at the two men.

"That's a helpful bit of information you've given me," he said. "There are tiny burn marks on both hands; I think there's not much doubt that he was electrocuted.

"If I may use your telephone, I'll inform the Coroner's Officer now. What's the deceased man's name?"

"John Kemp," replied Adrian. "Come through, please."

In the office, he indicated an empty desk. "You can use that telephone. The chap who sits there is out of the office meeting a client."

Neil and Margaret looked on curiously as Dr Atherton was occupied on the telephone for several minutes. Eventually he replaced the receiver and stood up.

"I've been lucky. The Coroner's Officer was at his desk in West End Central police station. He'll be here in ten minutes. I told him about the kettle, and no doubt the coroner will want to have it checked by a competent electrician. That's as much as I can do for you." With a courteous 'good day', Dr Atherton left.

Barely any time passed before a middle-aged police constable arrived. Far from having the lugubrious face that the office occupants had subconsciously expected of someone who was daily involved with death, this man had a beaming smile and a friendly manner.

"My name is Banks," he announced, "here on the orders of Mr Wilson, the Coroner, to see about the deceased."

Once again, Adrian and Martin assumed joint responsibility and showed the officer into the kitchen. Constable Banks had no need to look at the body for long.

"As Dr Atherton has confirmed the man is dead, even though he won't give a certificate, Mr Wilson says we can move the body to the Middlesex Hospital morgue. Then I'm to get the police surgeon to do a *post mortem* as soon as possible.

"I'll take the kettle and get that looked at, as Doc Atherton seems to think it's to blame."

Constable Banks picked up the suspected cause of the trouble with its cord still connected.

"I'll get the undertakers to come and remove the deceased as soon as possible – should be within a couple of hours.

"In the old days, an inquest jury would put a deodand on this kettle," was his parting remark as he left the office, "but I reckon the value wouldn't be very high!" With another smile and a cheery 'farewell to one and all', the coroner's representative left.

Julian Webb, when given the latest news, seemed more annoyed by the loss of the kettle than by the loss of a member of his staff. He promptly repeated his earlier remark that Margaret should go out and buy a new kettle – whichever model she thought was best.

Margaret agreed. She made coffee for the four men, courtesy of the office next door, and then escaped into Oxford Street where she bought a new electric kettle – this time in chromed rather than bare copper. Happy with her choice, she took her own coffee break in Selfridge's café.

Whilst she was out, a local firm of undertakers came to remove the body. By the time Margaret returned, the little firm had reverted to something approaching normal.

Julian Webb summoned Adrian to discuss how the remaining five members of the team could share John's work.

"It's not going to be easy," said Adrian. "John was working with two different clients, more-or-less on his own. Neither Martin nor I have the time to take them on unless we can drop something else.

"Harry could either take over one client, or perhaps take both and ease off on his other work. But, as Harry doesn't always get on with people, you might not want to risk his antagonising the Lazenby people, who loved John to the extent that he had them eating out of his hand.

"And in my opinion, Neil simply isn't ready

to take on a major client again yet, even under close supervision – although I don't doubt he'll try to persuade you otherwise.

"Ideally, I think you need to replace John, preferably with an experienced man."

"Agreed," replied Webb. "Draw up an advert – you know the sort of thing – and get it into the Standard and the News. Probably too late for tomorrow's editions, but as soon as possible anyway.

"Also, and this is a bit of a long shot, go round yourself to that Brook Street Bureau place in the morning, and ask if they can help. Try to see the manager – Mrs Berney. I've heard she is very efficient at finding people for various posts.

"If she can't produce an experienced ad man, see if she has a bright, well-educated temp, who could help us out with all our routine stuff for a week or two. That would at least free up the rest of us a bit to keep John's work ticking over."

Adrian confirmed he would enlist the agency's help. Leaving his boss' office he found that everyone else had already gone for lunch, and decided he would do the same. Julian could answer the phone if it rang.

****

Wednesday 31st August 1949

The following morning, there were fewer people in the office than usual. John was dead, and Mr Webb wasn't expected until after lunch if at all. Adrian had gone to Brook Street, and Harry was visiting another client. Neil was, as usual, late; Martin and Margaret were the sole representatives of Julian Webb & Co.

At 9:15, the office door opened, and two men came in. The taller man introduced them both:

"I'm Detective Chief Inspector Bryce, and this is Detective Sergeant Haig. We're here regarding the death of John Kemp."

Martin and Margaret gave their names and explained why they were alone in the office that morning. The DCI asked for the absentees' names, and Sergeant Haig noted these in his pocketbook.

"Show us where the incident took place, please," said Bryce.

Martin led the two officers into the kitchen.

"Last thing the Coroner's Officer said was 'in the old days the jury would have put a deodand on the kettle'," remarked Martin. "I had no idea what a deodand was, so after he'd gone I looked it up in the office Britannica."

"That makes two of us, Mr Lawn – I havenae any idea either," said Sergeant Haig.

Bryce, who was looking at the new kettle and the power socket in the wall, spoke without turning around.

"A deodand, Sergeant, means a thing 'given to God' – in English law an object forfeited because it caused a person's death.

"It could be an animate object, say a

runaway horse, or an inanimate object like a haystack or, as happened later, a machine. There were various complications, but the basic idea was that the offending item was sold.

"Originally, the proceeds went to the Crown, and thence supposedly to some good cause. In later years, the jury would decide the value, and the owner effectively paid that amount in damages to injured parties.

"When railways began to appear across the country, inquest juries started to apply the old law after railway accidents, because there was limited recourse to compensation for those who had suffered loss.

"It came to a head in 1841, when one of Brunel's Great Western Railway engines, 'Hecla', ploughed into a landslip in a cutting. Eight passengers, travelling in what was by today's standards really only a goods train, were killed. The coroner's jury laid a deodand of £1000 on the engine and train – an immense sum for the time.

"Later, the Board of Enquiry exonerated the railway, and the sum was greatly reduced on appeal."

Martin, having never seen the DCI before, was impressed. Sergeant Haig was unsurprised – knowing that his boss loved railway history, had a law degree, and possessed an excellent memory besides.

"But as a direct result, really, Parliament did two things," continued Bryce, looking around the rest of the room as he spoke, "in 1846, deodands were abolished, and the Fatal Accidents Act was passed, providing for compensation to be paid to relatives of victims. The early railway companies didn't like deodands, but I believe they fought against the idea of compensation even harder.

"As it's just over a hundred years since deodands were abolished, I'm a bit surprised to hear mention of them today!"

Bryce, having finished his inspection of the new kettle and kitchen, turned to Martin.

"But in any case, Mr Lawn, I'm afraid that even if that old law still prevailed, a deodand wouldn't have been appropriate in this case. It wasn't a faulty kettle which killed Mr Kemp. He was murdered. Somebody has deliberately tampered with the electric plug – 'with malice aforethought', as the saying goes."

Martin stared at Bryce in amazement.

"Oh God," he blurted. After thinking for a few seconds, he added "I thought it was a bit odd for a policeman of your rank coming to look into an accidental death, but now it makes sense.

"Look," he continued, "you'll obviously want to talk to all of us. Our boss, Mr Webb, isn't here this morning, and may not come in at all today. But I'm sure he wouldn't mind if you used his office for the time being."

"Thank you, Mr Lawn, very helpful. There's nothing for us to see here, so lead on, if you please. And we may as well start with you."

As they passed through the main office, Bryce smiled at Margaret.

"We'll just have a brief chat with your colleague here, and then perhaps you can talk to us," he said.

The inner office contained several chairs for visitors. Rather than sitting in Webb's own seat, Bryce placed a chair to one side of the desk, and Haig another on the opposite side, his pocketbook open on the desk beside him.

"Pull up another chair," instructed the DCI. "We have your names, so give us your address and tell us about yourself, and about the firm, Mr Lawn."

Martin, his mind still racing at the unexpected news he had been given, sat down in front of the desk, looking alternately at Haig and Bryce.

"Well," he said at last, "I live at 145 Andover Street, NW. I'm 32, and single. I took a degree in English here in London and I'd just graduated when the war came. I served in the Navy throughout, and after demob tried out a different job for a year before I came here.

"Julian Webb & Co is an advertising agency. We're small, but successful, well thought of, and expanding steadily. We have several very well-known clients on our books.

"Mr Webb – Julian Webb – owns the firm, of course. I assume he and his wife are the only shareholders, but I don't know that for a fact. He's a really good employer, and although he's a stickler for detail – pernickety, really – everyone likes him."

"A good start, Mr Lawn, thank you," said Bryce. "Just a very brief sketch now of the other people who work here."

Martin marshalled his thoughts as Sergeant Haig sharpened his pencil.

"The senior man in the office – 'team leader' is what Mr Webb calls him – is Adrian Hunter. He joined the firm immediately after the war, when Mr Webb was starting up. They had both served together as pilots in the RAF, apparently. He's another very good man – steady, sensible, and always fair.

"Harry Giles wasn't here yesterday, as he was away visiting a client in Birmingham, and isn't due back until tomorrow. In many ways he's a lovely chap, and I get on with him very well.

"However, not everyone he meets feels the same. If he doesn't like someone – almost at first sight – he can actually become quite unpleasant. He isn't as well educated as the rest of us, but he's a born salesman. He could sell anything from brushes to barnacles door-to-door, and do very well at it. It's just his knack – new clients feel convinced they need Webb and Co to handle their business after he's canvassed them. Harry accepts that he isn't particularly literate, and is perfectly happy for one of us to help him when it comes to writing up reports, or whatever. I think, in time, Harry will exclusively handle marketing of the firm's services and winning new accounts for Julian."

Martin paused, concerned in case he wasn't responding in the manner required.

"Is this the sort of information you're after, Chief Inspector?" he asked.

"Oh yes, Mr Lawn, it's exactly what we want; do carry on please," replied Bryce.

"Well, next is Mrs Margaret Collins – she's the one outside now. Joined the firm soon after I came. Lovely lady, very competent. A war widow. She isn't a secretary or general clerk; she's employed on the same basis as the rest of us. In fact we all generally do our own typing, filing, and so on, and if it's anything lengthy we bring in an agency typist.

"It was Margaret who found the body this morning. Quite a shock for her, I fear.

"Then we come to Neil Hazel," continued Martin. "I'll tell you now that I don't like the man. He has a very high opinion of himself. And I for one don't share that opinion. It's believed that he got the job through some obscure Webb family connection. He's the junior member of the team – but for some reason treats Margaret like a skivvy.

"The fact is that she's far more intelligent than he is, but because he has a degree and she hasn't, he lords it over her. I did point out once that it was considerably easier for a man to go to university in 1945 than for a woman in the early 1930s, but he just sneered. I tried to press him on his own university laurels recently, but he clammed up. My guess – and I know I'm being very catty – is that he got a third in divinity.

"His written English is certainly nothing to boast about – it always needs a lot of editing and, worse than that, he simply doesn't have an awareness of what to steer clear of when he's creating copy. In fact, you may have seen one of his slogans a while back – for the Lighter Bread Company?"

Haig's explosive snort of laughter suggested that he had come across it, but Bryce shook his head. Fixing a quizzical gaze on his DS he said:

"I'm intrigued, Sergeant. Care to explain the joke?"

"The advertisements didnae stay up long, sir, which is probably why you never saw them. The original wording was four short lines of doggerel,

> To be well fed
> Buy Lighter Bread
> Won't leave you feeling
> Like you've eaten lead.

"Some wit realised from the way the poster was printed that he could add an additional two lines in what looked exactly like the original writing,

> Leaves you all blown up
> And full of wind instead!

"Some clever but rude sketches were added, to make the new message even clearer. Almost overnight, it seemed every poster got the same treatment."

Bryce laughed, but Martin Lawn looked mortified.

"Absolutely dreadful, awful, advertisement! I still don't understand how Mr Webb ever approved it. I think he must have wanted to give Neil some encouragement, but even so, the potential for defacing the ad was self-evident from the outset.

"Naturally, I had to do another one, gratis, for the Lighter Bread Company. That's the one up at the moment."

"Aye, well that's a good replacement," said Haig. "Might even ask Fiona to risk buying some Lighter bread now!"

"That's certainly an insight into some of the pitfalls of advertising and office dynamics you've given us," said Bryce. "Does make you question whether PT Barnum was right when he said, 'there's no such thing as bad publicity'. Carry on, please."

"Because of what John was doing when he died, I suppose you should know about our roster for making coffee and so on. All of us – even Mr Webb – take turns in doing that. If someone has an outside appointment on 'their' day, they arrange a swap with someone else. Today it was John's turn. When he didn't come back with the coffee, Margaret went to see where he was."

"You're doing very well, Mr Lawn," said Bryce. "My Sergeant and I are getting a very clear picture. Now, just a quick outline of the dead man, please."

"John was another nice chap. A tad eccentric, but in the most harmless ways. For example, whether he was on coffee duty or not, he invariably went into the kitchen every morning to make himself some toast. He seemed to have a different type of marmalade on it each day. Until yesterday he had an ancient electric toaster, and it sometimes burnt his toast. He apparently spent a small fortune on a replacement automatic toaster, which he used this morning. However, he died before he could eat today's output.

"You'll be wanting his address, and so on, but I can't help you there. Adrian Hunter said this morning that he was single and lived in Leytonstone; the actual address will be in Mr Webb's files somewhere, no doubt.

"Thank you very much, Mr Lawn," said Bryce. "Any reason you can think of why someone would want to kill Mr Kemp?"

"None whatsoever, Chief Inspector," replied Martin. "A more inoffensive man it would be hard to find.

"And murder? Really? I just can't see that. Yes, Adrian and I thought he might have been electrocuted and the doctor seemed to agree, but we assumed accidental death – a fault on the kettle. The fuse had blown, in fact. It was only a 5 Amp fuse, and since the kettle was rated at one kilowatt, it could have blown at any time.

"Something else seemed to confirm the kettle fault. After I replaced the fuse, and plugged the kettle in again, it still didn't work, although the fuse didn't blow a second time."

"You plugged it in again, did you," said Bryce, thoughtfully. "Describe in detail what you did before and after mending the fuse and returning to the kitchen."

Martin paused to think.

"The kettle was already full of water, standing beside the sink. Before I went to deal with the fuse, I pulled the plug from the wall socket, but left the other end in the kettle. After mending the fuse, I simply took the plug and inserted it into the wall socket.

"I was distracted for a bit as Adrian came to talk about getting a doctor, and then I realised that the kettle still wasn't boiling. I think it simultaneously dawned on Adrian and me that the faulty kettle and John's death could be connected. Adrian carefully unplugged the kettle from the wall, and nobody touched it again until the police constable took it away."

"I think you've been remarkably lucky, Mr Lawn," said Bryce. "Mr Hunter, too.

"You see, the wall plug on the end of the kettle flex had been tampered with, so that when it was plugged into the mains the body of the kettle became live. The earth lead was disconnected. When you replaced the fuse and plugged the kettle in again, it would have been live – and potentially lethal – again."

Martin was staring at the Yard detectives in amazement.

"But don't you have to touch two things to get an electric shock?" he asked."

"Yes," said Sergeant Haig. "If you touched the kettle and were making a good contact with the earth – standing barefoot on a wet floor, for example – that would be enough. But a better chance of getting a shock would be to touch the kettle with one hand and a tap with the other. That's what the doctor thinks happened with Mr Kemp."

"It wouldn't have to be the tap, though," said Bryce. "The casing of that shiny new toaster will be earthed, so touching the kettle with one hand and the toaster with the other..."

"Martin was still thinking. "Well, I can see that Adrian and I are both fortunate to be here, as you say. But couldn't the wires in the plug have somehow become twisted or something? I mean, it's impossible for me to believe that someone did this deliberately."

"No, Mr Lawn, there is no shadow of doubt about this. The earth was disconnected, and the earth wire in the flex deliberately connected to the live pin.

"So, one final question. Apart from those who work here, who else has access to this kitchen?"

"Easy question, Chief Inspector," replied Martin, still shaken. "There's a cleaner who comes in to do the office on Tuesdays and Thursdays. I suppose she does the kitchen too, but because she comes after we've gone home, I've never actually seen her. In fact, I'm only assuming it's a woman. I don't think anyone else ever goes into the kitchen."

"Good. Thank you, Mr Lawn. We'll let you go now."

As the ad man rose to leave, Bryce joined him at the door and preceded him into the outer office, ensuring he didn't speak to Margaret.

"Mrs Collins, I wonder if we can have our little chat now?" said Bryce.

Margaret sat in the chair vacated by Martin. In her late thirties, Bryce and Haig had no difficulty believing the description Lawn had given was correct. Her face and demeanour shouted 'I may be a woman in a man's world, but I'm as good as any of them; and better than quite a few'.

"Sorry to interrupt your work, Mrs Collins, but this is a serious matter, and we need to get to the bottom of it," Bryce began.

"You worry me, Chief Inspector," Margaret interposed. "I've read about you in the papers. I understood that poor John died from a faulty kettle. Surely a tragic accident doesn't require investigation by Scotland Yard's crack team of detectives?"

Bryce smiled faintly. "Sergeant Haig and I appreciate the appellation – not to say accolade," he replied. "However, as I've already explained to Mr Lawn, I'm afraid the death, although tragic, was certainly not an accident. The kettle plug had been tampered with. We are investigating a clear case of murder."

Margaret nodded slowly. "I see," she said, "so one of us is guilty of killing poor John. When I found him on the floor, I assumed he'd had a heart attack. That was shock enough. Then we learned he'd been electrocuted, which at least was more understandable than having a heart attack at his age. But now," she shuddered, and her cheeks lost quite a bit of their colour, "well, it's not understandable at all."

"I suppose murders could be split into two categories," said Sergeant Haig, unusually philosophical. "With some, the motive is quite obvious to any onlooker. With the other sort, it's almost impossible for anyone to understand the reasoning behind the murderer's decision to kill, even after he or she has been identified."

Bryce smiled at Haig's remark, thinking that his Sergeant was getting much better at speaking up.

"That's quite right," he agreed. "Now, Mr Lawn has told us that he can't think of a single reason why anyone should dislike let alone kill Mr

Kemp, so this murder may well be one of those in Sergeant Haig's second category.

"Can you offer a motive for anyone, Mrs Collins?"

"I don't even need to think about it, Chief Inspector; the answer is a loud and resounding 'no'. We do have a rather obnoxious young man in the office, but I wouldn't dream of suggesting that he would commit murder."

"Ah, that would be Mr Hazel, I assume?" asked Bryce.

Mrs Collins wasn't at all put out that she had been presented with the name that she hadn't wanted to give herself.

"Correct," she said. "And since you could only have heard about him from Martin, I'm glad that I'm not the only one who doesn't give Neil full marks for being a human being!

"But seriously, Chief Inspector, nobody here would have any reason to dislike John, let alone to kill him."

"Who else might have access to the kitchen?" asked Haig.

"Well, we have occasional visitors, but I don't remember any of them ever going into the kitchen – whoever has invited them would normally fetch refreshments, unless of course the visit coincided with a routine coffee break, in which case the person on coffee duty that day would include the visitor, of course.

"We do have a cleaner who comes in twice a

week – dusts, empties wastepaper baskets, and so on. I imagine she goes into the kitchen as well. I've only seen her a couple of times. She's a homely old soul. I believe she 'does' for several other offices in this building, and perhaps elsewhere.

"But as for her having the knowledge to tamper with electrics, I just can't see it. Anyway, she doesn't know us, except perhaps by sight. John was never one for working late, so I'd bet that she's never even seen him."

"Fair enough, but we'll have to speak to her, of course. You presumably don't have her details yourself?"

"No – her name is Olive, but I have no idea of surname or address. You'll have to ask Mr Webb. She would have been here last night, of course, so she won't be in again until tomorrow."

"One last question, Mrs Collins. Who has keys to the office?"

"I think we all do, Chief Inspector," Margaret replied. "The idea is that if one of us is returning after a visit to a client, and it's past normal finishing time, we can still get in to drop off papers or whatever. Also, some of us occasionally come in on a Saturday or even a Sunday, to work on a project – I do, for one.

She thought for a moment. "Obviously Olive has a key too, and I suppose if she wanted, she could arrange to let some maniac borrow it. I can't see that, though – but then I can't see any of my colleagues doing it either.

"Can you tell how much technical knowledge would have been required to do whatever it is?"

"Not very much, really – just a basic understanding of the functions of the different wires in a three-core flex. Anyone who does simple home maintenance – fitting a plug onto a new electrical appliance, for example – would have been able to fix this."

"I see," said Margaret. "Well, I have to admit that I can do that. After I lost my husband, I had to learn how to do several little jobs which might traditionally be thought of as 'man's work'."

"Don't worry, Mrs Collins," said Bryce, standing up to indicate the interview was over. "We look for 'means, motive, and opportunity'. Stretching a point, we might include the ability to wire a plug in the 'means' category. But to start with we'll concentrate more on 'motive'."

Opening the door to the main office, Margaret realised that Neil was now at his desk. Turning back to the police officers, she passed on the information. This time Haig got up and went to the door.

"Mr Hazel, I believe?" he said.

Neil agreed that he was. "We are police officers," continued the Sergeant, "looking into the death of Mr Kemp. Perhaps you can spare a few minutes."

Neil took his turn in the chair facing the Yard detectives.

For a few moments they all looked at each other. The officers appraised their interviewee. He was an attractive young man in his mid-twenties. Wearing a good quality dark grey suit in a discreet pin stripe, a white shirt, again with a faint stripe, and what might have been – but wasn't – a Guards' tie, he was extremely well turned-out. But in reading his face, both Bryce and Haig quite independently thought of the same word – sly.

"Now, Mr Hazel, what can you tell us about yesterday's incident," began the DCI.

"I can't tell you anything, really," replied Neil. "John didn't come back with the coffee. Margaret went to see why not. Came back. Told us he was dead. Passed out on the floor. A bit later we heard that he'd had an electric shock from a faulty kettle. That's the sum total of my knowledge."

Neither detective was impressed with Hazel's delivery, least of all the sneering manner in which he described Mrs Collins' reaction on discovering John Kemp. Before Bryce could put his next question, Neil spoke again:

"But, I say, aren't you making a mountain out of a molehill here? What has a broken kettle got to do with the police? The inquest will inevitably just say 'accidental death'. And the kettle was so old that I hardly think the Bulpitt people will bear any responsibility for what happened. It's just one of those things."

Bryce looked steadily at Neil for a few moments and pointedly didn't respond to the question, putting his own instead:

"Did you like Mr Kemp?"

"I neither liked nor disliked him," replied Hazel coolly. "I didn't have much to do with him, actually. He was odd – had some very funny habits."

"Like eating toast and marmalade every morning?" queried Haig.

"Yes, you've obviously heard about that. But there were other things too. For example, he has a pipe rack on his desk. Nothing unusual about that, perhaps – but there is a Monday pipe, a Tuesday pipe, and so on. Before we knew he was dead this morning, Adrian speculated that he also had a different marmalade for each day of the weekend, too."

"But nothing in these eccentricities to make you actively dislike him?" asked Bryce."

"Not as such, no. But if you're looking to push me on the point, I'd say he wasn't the sort that I'd have wanted to go for a drink with every Friday after work, and leave it at that," replied Neil.

There was another long pause, both officers looking hard at the young man in front of them. Neil began to fidget under their gaze, but said no more.

Eventually, Bryce spoke again.

"You are quite wrong about the inquest verdict, Mr Hazel. John Kemp was murdered. We're here to find out who did it."

Neil half rose from his chair, with a look

on his face which combined astonishment and horror, and then sank back again.

"Careful you don't fold up on the floor in fright," advised Sergeant Haig sarcastically.

Hazel shot him a furious glance, but said nothing.

When neither policeman said anything further, Neil blurted out:

"But Adrian and Martin said it was the kettle. And I heard the doctor talking on the telephone to the coroner or someone – he said the same!

"Murder – are you saying he was poisoned or stabbed or something?"

Bryce chose to respond now, "Oh no, Mr Hazel, he was electrocuted right enough. It's just that someone decided to tamper with the kettle's flex in order to kill him."

"No, no! You can't have that right, it must have been an accident," babbled Neil.

"Let me assure you that it very definitely wasn't an accident. Now, just tell us what you know about electricity and plugs and wires and so on," said Bryce.

"You can't pin this on me!" shouted Neil.

"Be quiet!" barked the DCI sharply. "I'm not trying to pin this on you or anybody else at the moment. But we have to explore all the possibilities. Now, just answer the question."

Neil subsided. He sat still; his hands clasped tightly together in his lap.

"I know enough to put a plug onto a household electrical item," he said at last. "I've watched my Dad do it a few times. But I've never actually done it myself. I know which wires are live, neutral, and earth, but I suppose almost everyone knows that."

"I doubt that very much, Mr Hazel," remarked Haig. "I think the only things the average person knows about electricity are that it's invisible and it's dangerous – the good servant and terrible master. Most people are very wary of it."

Neil nodded reluctantly, and seemed to be calm again.

"But how could someone use electricity to kill John?" he asked.

"Quite simple, really," replied Bryce. "The plug had been rewired so that the body of the kettle became live as soon as the kettle was plugged in. Mr Kemp touched the kettle, and at the same time touched something that was earthed – tap, toaster, or whatever."

"Oh God," said Neil. "This is awful. You obviously think one of us in the office did it."

"Well, someone did it," said Haig, "and there don't seem to be many outside candidates, apart from a cleaner who has probably never even seen Mr Kemp."

Neil was released, and through the open office door Bryce could see that two more men – Adrian and Harry – had arrived. Inevitably, Martin and Margaret had told both of them the situation. Harry, who had been absent the whole of yesterday, was astounded to learn that John was dead at all; whilst Adrian had still been assuming the death was an accident. He too was horrified to learn the facts.

Over the next twenty minutes, the new arrivals were called for interview. Adrian could add nothing more to the report given by Martin.

Harry took his turn and sat down opposite the two detectives. He was short in stature, balding, with horn-rimmed spectacles. He wore a tweed jacket and flannel trousers. Bryce guessed him to be about fifty. Evidently still shocked by what he had been told a few minutes before, he seemed unable to comprehend the questions put to him, although he did manage to confirm that he could think of nobody who would have any reason to kill John. In saying that tears welled up in his eyes.

"Were you friends with Mr Kemp, outside the office?" asked Haig.

Harry looked at him, apparently trying to understand.

"No," he said eventually. "I did like John, perhaps partly because he was a bit different, like me. To be honest, I don't really have friends. I like most of the people in the office here, and get on well with them at work. I get on okay with most clients too, but I'll admit that there are some people I just can't stand. There's no logic to it; it's just so. I've always been that way. Mr Webb knows all about my problem, but he says I'm very good at the job when I do like a client. He reckons he can afford to accept that sometimes another agent has to take over one of my clients, and unruffle feathers."

Listening to Harry, Bryce thought of Martin Lawn's description of him as a 'born salesman', and struggled to see any sign of that in the man before him. But he didn't discount the depiction, realising that the news must have significantly affected Harry's normal demeanour. And if Webb was prepared to overlook a certain amount of disruptive behaviour, clearly there must be a great deal more to Giles than was on display at the moment.

Anyway, since Harry hadn't been present during the incident the previous day, he obviously couldn't tell the officers any more about it.

"Thank you for your help, Mr Giles," concluded Bryce.

Leaving the inner office with Giles, Bryce walked over to Adrian Hunter's desk and asked him to telephone the boss at his home.

"If Mr Webb is there, I'd like you to explain the latest development, and ask if he could provide the name of the cleaner or the company she works for. Would you also ask him to confirm if he's coming into the office later today or tomorrow? Perhaps best if you also warn him that his office has been commandeered."

The DCI returned to the inner office, closed

the door, and sat down for a discussion with his Sergeant.

"Thoughts so far?" he asked.

"Odd bunch, these advertising people," replied Haig. "To be quite honest, sir, Mr Giles comes across as not being the full shilling; and Mr Hazel strikes me as being untrustworthy, as well as being full of himself. We didn't meet the dead man, but he seems to have been odd in his ways, too. It'll be interesting to see what the head man is like.

"But all that said, sir, everyone seems to have liked Mr Kemp. I've heard nothing at all to suggest a motive, and no gut feeling telling me that any particular suspect is guilty."

"Agreed," said Bryce. "And eccentrics don't generally go around committing murder for no reason. Actually, I've never seen a murder by electrocution before, although there may have been a few. Probably some cases put down as 'accidents' were actually murders. As in this case, originally. If the Coroner's Officer had just thrown an apparently faulty kettle in the bin, rather than taking the trouble to get an electrician to see exactly why the kettle went wrong, we almost certainly wouldn't be here today.

"Even in fiction, it hasn't exactly been a popular method," said Bryce thoughtfully. "I can only think of three examples amongst hundreds of fictional murders. One was totally unfeasible, and the other two wildly improbable.

"Here, if it wasn't for the crystal-clear

evidence from the kettle plug, which we've both seen with our own eyes, one could hardly believe this is a murder case either. And, not for the first time, we don't seem to have a motive."

The two officers sat in contemplation for a few minutes, until there was a knock on the door and Adrian poked his head into the room.

"He was at home, Chief Inspector. I thought he was having apoplexy or something when I gave him the news – he just made spluttering noises for a minute. He doesn't remember the cleaner's name except that she's Olive. But he says if it's urgent there is a file in the bottom drawer of the left-hand filing cabinet marked 'cleaning'. The information will be in there.

"But he's coming in immediately in any case. He lives out at Moor Park – likes his golf. It's a hell of a journey, about ten stops on the Metropolitan Line, and another two on the Bakerloo, but I guess he'll be here in an hour or so. He says you are welcome to use the office for as long as you're here, provided he can nip in and collect a file or something if he needs it."

Bryce thanked Adrian, and when the door closed behind him, he and Haig looked at each other.

"I have to confess that I don't see what else we can do for the moment, Sergeant," said Bryce. "We'd better try to see this Olive, although I don't hold out any hope there. Have a look in that cabinet and see if you can find the cleaning file."

"Got it, sir," reported Haig a minute later. He quickly scanned through the papers.

"Olive Spurdin. She doesn't seem to work for a company, just for herself. Mr Webb engaged her following a recommendation from two other offices in this building. There's an address in Walthamstow."

"I don't want to wait around here until late in the evening. See if you can find a detective constable at the Yard. Tell him to take a car, go to Walthamstow, and bring Mrs Spurdin here as soon as possible if she's available. We'll also take her home again, of course.

"When you've finished, get them to put you back to the Yard switchboard – I want talk to the fingerprint people."

Sergeant Haig completed this task within two minutes, and handed the telephone to his boss.

"Sergeant Beck? DCI Bryce here. That electric kettle and flex you were given earlier. Anything to report yet?"

Beck spoke loudly and clearly, and Haig was sitting close enough to Bryce to hear his response.

"The kettle is covered in prints, sir, as is the outside of the plug which was tampered with, although they're all overlapping and blurry there. When I undid the plug, there was nothing to pick up inside. Matter of fact, there's not really any surface to leave prints on inside, but it's clean anyway.

"None of the prints we have found are in our records. Sorry we can't be more use, sir."

"Never mind Sergeant, not your fault, thanks anyway."

Bryce put down the telephone, and looked at Haig.

"Do you want me to take everyone's prints, sir?" asked the Sergeant.

"No, I really don't think it's worthwhile. All of our suspects legitimately handled the kettle at some time or other. And given that neither kettle nor plug has a built-in switch, everyone wanting to turn the kettle off must have done it by pulling the plug from the wall socket, or the plug from the kettle. And the reverse for turning it on, of course. So, we could expect everyone's prints to be on the plug too."

Bryce consulted his watch. "It's gone half past eleven. Neither Mrs Spurdin nor Mr Webb can realistically get here for the best part of an hour, so let's go and get a bite to eat. There's a Lyon's in Oxford Street a little way past the tube station – can't be more than three hundred yards. I'll buy you an early lunch – or a brunch."

Haig looked enthusiastic at the proposal.

Bryce told the staff that he and the Sergeant would be back inside an hour, and the two men made their way down Regent Street, turned left at Oxford Circus and crossed the road to the Lyons café.

Consulting the menu, both men opted for

sausages and chipped potatoes. To follow, Bryce chose trifle, and Haig fruit jelly. Each ordered a pot of tea. Bryce handed over four shillings, and the officers carried their trays to a convenient table.

As usual, they discussed general topics whilst eating – the current position with food and other rationing; the recent disappointing drawn test series, and the reasons why there was to be no winter cricket tour this year.

Their meal over, they walked back to Great Castle Street, and re-established themselves in Mr Webb's office.

Within minutes, there was a sudden tap on the door, which opened before either officer could call 'come in'. A shortish man breezed in and put his hand out first to Haig, who happened to be nearer, and then to Bryce.

"Well, gentlemen, I'm Julian Webb," the newcomer announced. "This is a terrible and unbelievable business."

Bryce indicated that Webb should sit in his own chair, and he and Haig moved their chairs to face him.

Webb was a man in his mid-thirties, with very fair, neatly trimmed hair. The most striking thing about him was a huge 'handlebar' moustache, of the type popular among RAF officers during the war. Although looking harassed, and dressed in casual clothes, he still contrived to appear smart.

"Adrian told me what has happened," said

Webb. "I took a taxi to get here as fast as I could – didn't even change, as you can see – although now I'm here I'm not at all sure what I can do to help. Can you please explain how this could possibly be murder?"

Bryce nodded to Haig, for him to answer.

"I'm afraid there's no doubt, sir. The plug at the wall end of the kettle flex had been deliberately tampered with, such that the live connection went straight to the metal casing of the kettle. The earth itself was disconnected. It's impossible that it could have happened by accident."

"Oh God, I see," said Webb.

Bryce took over:

"Mr Webb, we've heard from all your staff about what happened yesterday morning, and since the reports tally there isn't much point asking you about the incident itself.

"But perhaps you could tell us something about the individuals in the office – how they relate, what makes them tick, and so on."

"Yes, of course," replied Webb. "Obviously you're assuming that the culprit is one of us – and while I find that very hard to believe, I have to concede that I can't think of anyone else who ever goes into the kitchen. Except for Olive, of course – did you find her details, by the way?"

Bryce confirmed that not only had the details been found, but that the cleaner was currently being tracked down.

"Well," continued Webb, "let's see. This is

an advertising agency, as you presumably know. I started it at the end of the war. It's a partnership – my wife and I own eighty percent of the business, and Adrian Hunter owns the remainder. Only he, Anne and I are aware of Adrian's share, incidentally.

"I've known Adrian for a long time. We were both at university together, and then when the war came we both ended up in the same RAF squadron. I'd trust him with my life. Have done, actually.

"Martin Lawn is another good chap. Ex-Royal Navy, but I overlooked that shortcoming," said Webb with a faint smile. "Motor Torpedo Boats, I understand, so plenty of guts. He joined us a couple of years ago, and I have absolutely no complaint about his work. He, Adrian and I are all of an age, of course.

"Margaret Collins is another really excellent employee. A little older, and in many ways a good deal wiser. 'Quietly competent' is the expression, I suppose. Her husband was killed in Burma.

"I assume you've talked to Harry Giles. He's the office elder, and isn't as well educated. Bit of a Jekyll and Hyde character in some ways. If he takes agin someone, he can be really difficult – nasty, even – for no apparent reason. It follows that he takes a bit of managing when it comes to allocating work. However, we've never had any problems with behaviour in the office here. But when the rest of us occasionally have a meal together out of hours, Harry chooses not to be included. He isn't a social animal.

"Lastly, we have Neil Hazel. He is, between ourselves, a big disappointment. I only took him on because he is distantly related to my wife. He isn't as bright as he thinks, he doesn't work as hard as any of the others, and he believes he's better than anyone else – particularly Margaret, who is remarkably tolerant of his practice of treating her like the office dogsbody. I overheard him talking to her last week, and I've been waiting for a suitable time to take it up with him. Frankly, it's likely that I'll dismiss him, although with John gone as well it'll really be a strain on the firm, particularly as we've been growing rapidly.

"Yesterday, I asked Adrian to try to find – or at least advertise for – an experienced marketing person to replace John. When you've finished with me, I'll see how he has got on. It'll be far easier to replace Neil if that becomes necessary – almost anyone one straight out of university, or even with a good Higher Certificate, could do as well as he does. So long as they have that certain flair with words that Neil really doesn't. It's one of those innate attributes; you've either got it or you haven't."

"Tell us about the roster for 'coffee prefect', or whatever you call it," said Bryce.

Webb laughed. "It's been going for about a year. Before that, everyone made their own whenever they felt like it. It wasn't very efficient.

I think it was Martin who suggested a formal system, everyone taking turns. I thought it was sensible, and offered to include myself in the new arrangement.

"A few days before the end of each month, Margaret draws up the list for the following month. She volunteered, by the way. We have our own diaries, of course, but there is also a general office diary, where each of us enters forthcoming away meetings with clients, so if someone isn't here we know where they are and when they are due back. Margaret takes those diary entries into account when she prepares the roster – and she pins the finished version up on the notice board.

"But, of course, new appointments are inevitably made later. So, the agreement is that if someone needs to be out when it's his or her turn, then they must arrange a substitute. That probably happens several times each month.

"I note my own coffee days in my own diary, but otherwise I neither know nor care who is on duty on any particular day."

"We heard from someone that you sometimes bring in agency personnel, for typing and so on?" asked Haig. "When does that happen?"

"That's quite right, Sergeant," replied Webb. "We don't employ a clerk or secretary. We tend to do most of our own secretarial work – managing our own diaries, simple typing, and so on. Even I sometimes do a bit of typing.

"But quite often someone has something

either more complex, or more urgent, or perhaps something which needs a flawless professional presentation. Every member of staff may call in an agency temp – they don't need to ask for consent.

"For some months now, we've used the Lockwood agency, just around the corner. A couple of their girls, Gwen and Patty – Patricia – are quite regular visitors here, and they're both efficient.

"Patty was here last Friday, working for me, but as far as I know there was nobody from the agency here either on Monday or yesterday. You'd need to check with the others on that, of course.

"But I understand that even people like Patty and Gwen who are working here are still treated as visitors, and so they are brought a drink by the coffee person on duty. They wouldn't ever need to go into the kitchen."

"Do they have keys to the office, like your own staff?" asked Bryce.

"Certainly not," Webb replied. "In fact, it would be a breach of the lease to allow a temporary member of staff to have a key to the outer door anyway.

"The doorman downstairs goes off duty at six thirty, which is why my people have keys – if they're working late, they can lock the building on departure. Or, if they need to come in – say at a weekend – they can do that too."

"Very useful, Mr Webb, thank you," said Bryce. "What happens about refreshments in the afternoon?"

"Good question," replied Webb. "There isn't a formal arrangement at all, largely because for some reason nobody seems to take afternoon tea. Occasionally, one or two people, if they haven't gone out to lunch, might make a hot drink at lunchtime, but I think that would be exceptional – normally everyone leaves the office.

"But we don't generally work late. I don't expect it of my staff – I suppose I'm a bit unusual for a boss. People start going home soon after four pm, so there's not much call for tea at three o'clock."

"I see. Well, many thanks, Mr Webb. We're hoping to see Olive Spurdin soon, so we'll just stay here for a bit longer if that won't disrupt you too much."

"That won't be problem, Chief Inspector. This whole thing is so baffling. Nobody disliked John at all, never mind wanting to kill him. Anyway, if anything else comes to mind I'll certainly tell you."

Left on their own, the two officers looked at each other.

"Absence of motive," said Haig. "Worrying."

"Indeed," replied the DCI. "Let's look at means and opportunity instead. The kettle was used on Monday without mishap. Unless someone came in very early to tamper with the plug yesterday morning, it looks as though the scene was set after working hours on Monday evening. On a day when the cleaner wasn't here, it seems –

unless she is responsible, of course.

"We need to find out who might have stayed late, or come in later, and if possible who couldn't have done so – for example if he'd been in Glasgow or something."

"Yes, sir," said Haig. "Perhaps tomorrow I should ask around the other offices in the building, and find out if anyone happened to see someone coming in here. Pity the doorman isn't here twenty-four hours a day."

"Yes, try that by all means, Sergeant. But the chances are slim, I think – especially if the visit occurred very late. It's possible that Mrs Spurdin was around, of course, but if she was cleaning in another office there is little chance that she'd have seen someone coming in here."

"What about these Lockwood girls, sir?"

"We can't eliminate them yet, but I really can't see how they could possibly be involved," Bryce answered. "No, my money is on one of the people in the next room."

"Assuming they get hold of Olive, we'll talk to her, send her on her way, and then call it a day.

"Tomorrow, we'll look at asking people if they have an alibi for the period of, say, four pm on Monday afternoon to nine am on Tuesday morning."

The two talked over another, less serious case, for the next half hour until Julian Webb appeared at the door again, stepping aside to allow a woman into the room.

"This is Olive Spurdin," he announced. She was closely followed by a police officer in plain clothes. Webb withdrew, and closed the door behind him.

Haig and Bryce rose to welcome the newcomer. Bryce made the introductions and invited her to take a seat.

"Well done for finding Mrs Spurdin, Jackson. Sit yourself down over there," he instructed the detective constable.

Bryce and Haig assessed the cleaner, who looked straight back at them both and made her own assessment. She was slightly built and grey-haired, very plainly but tidily dressed, with lively brown eyes and an alert expression.

"First, Mrs Spurdin, thank you for coming," began Bryce. "Did Constable Jackson here explain anything about this business as he drove you here?"

"No sir, he didn't," replied the cleaner, her words quick and clipped. "But I didn't mind coming, 'cos I'd have been coming here tonight anyway. And I've never been shoofered anywhere before. Gave me a nice little taste of how the other 'alf lives!"

"Good. I'm glad we haven't inconvenienced you too much. Let me explain everything for you. Yesterday morning, in the kitchen here, one of Mr Webb's employees was killed by an electric shock. That death, unfortunate anyway, turns out to have been murder."

Olive looked stunned. "What's that got to do with me?" she squawked. "I wasn't here on Monday, nor yesterday until eight in the evening!"

"Nobody is blaming you for anything, Mrs Spurdin," replied Bryce reassuringly. "We're just talking to everyone who goes into the kitchen here."

"Well, I do. I don't deny it. Who's dead, and what's killed 'im?"

"The dead man is John Kemp, and he was killed when he got an electric shock from the kettle," said Bryce.

"Never heard of 'im," said Olive. "As for the kettle. I sometimes make myself a cup of tea of an evening. It's never killed me!"

"No, Mrs Spurdin, it didn't kill you because it hadn't been tampered with when you last used it," explained Bryce.

Olive stared back at the DCI, then nodded in understanding.

"Ah, that'd be it, sir. I did see last night that there was a new kettle. Didn't rightly like to use it in fact – not my place to christen it. But I s'pose what you're saying is I'd be less likely to die using that 'un?"

"Quite right, Mrs Spurdin," replied the DCI. "All we want to know is this: have you ever let anyone into this office in the evenings, perhaps someone who said he worked here but had forgotten his key, that sort of thing?"

"Never let anyone in, sir," she replied. "Never

been asked to, neither. I'm here eight to ten Tuesday and Thursday; it's the last office I do in this building both days. And I only ever see anyone in here maybe once every three or four months; that's either Mr Webb or that nice lady – Margaret, she told me her name is. That's several weeks since I saw either of them; I'd be hard pushed now to put any dates on when that was.

"But last night I did see someone else come in here. Not many minutes past ten it was. I was locking up my cupboard down the landing where my cleaning stuff is kept, and this chap came up the stairs, turned left, and went in this office. He didn't see me. I was at the far end of the landing and a long way past the light bulb near the stairs."

"Could you describe this man?" asked Haig.

"Only saw him from the back. Time I turned round he was unlocking the door and going in. Only thing I could tell for sure was it was a man."

There was silence for a minute.

Bryce looked at Haig to see if he had any further questions, and received a shake of the head.

"Thank you again, Mrs Spurdin," he said. "Do you want to have a lift back to Walthamstow? It's a bit of time before you start work, surely?"

"Not worth it, sir," replied the cleaner. "I'll hang around for a while."

Bryce dug in his pocket and extracted two half-crowns, which he gave to Olive, saying "Well, get yourself some supper before you start."

Olive took the coins happily,

"You can send your shoofer to pick me up any day, dearie, if this is the going rate!"

Haig and Jackson were both grinning broadly at this familiarity from the cleaner, and were pleased to see that Bryce was also amused.

With Olive gone, Bryce and Haig discussed her contribution to the investigation, Jackson listening in and picking up the threads of the case.

"It's a bit strange," said Bryce. "Once the victim was electrocuted, the culprit might reasonably assume that someone would throw the kettle out. But there must have been a serious risk that someone else would be hurt in the meantime – as it happened the fuse blew, but according to Mr Lawn that was partly because the fuse wire was of too low a rating. I don't think that could have been foreseen. So, if the kettle remained in situ, it would be sensible to restore the plug to its proper condition before someone came in to use the kettle the next day. There would still be a risk of someone using it again earlier of course; but if Webb is correct, nobody normally made a brew in the afternoon and rarely at lunchtime.

"So, unless the mystery man genuinely came in to work, I think it's probable that he came to see if the kettle was still here, and if so to restore the plug to normal."

"Mrs Spurdin knew Webb by sight, so even from the back she'd probably have recognised him. Who is your money on, Sergeant?"

"I wouldn't bet, sir. We've heard nothing to suggest any of them hated the man."

"That's right," said Bryce thoughtfully. "Something has just occurred to me. Nip next door, and ask for a copy of the current month's coffee rota."

Haig went into the main office, and Bryce could hear his request. He could also hear the replies, a bit of a jumble as at least three people spoke at once. "It's pinned up on the board over there" was the thrust.

Sergeant Haig returned to Mr Webb's office, and closed the door behind him. He handed the sheet to his boss.

"This may help to explain things," said Bryce, after looking at it. "According to this, Mr Kemp wasn't supposed to do the coffee thing yesterday – it was Neil Hazel. I'm putting my money on Harry Giles now.

Just ask Mr Hazel to pop in for a minute, please."

Haig called Neil in.

"Take a seat, Mr Hazel, although this'll only take a few seconds. Please explain why Mr Kemp was doing your coffee duty yesterday."

Neil looked at him in surprise.

"Good Lord, I'd forgotten that. Yes, he owed me a day, and about a week ago he offered to do my next day. It was agreed that he'd do yesterday. I noted it in my diary, and he must have done so too, but I suppose neither of us thought to alter the list pinned up on the notice board."

He suddenly jerked upright. "You think that if he hadn't swapped, I'd have been killed rather than John?"

"That seems a possibility, Mr Hazel," replied Bryce. "Now I want you to leave this room, and sit down at your desk without speaking or even looking at anyone. Get your head down over your work and keep it there. Understand?"

Neil indicated that he did.

"Ask Mr Giles to spare us a minute, Sergeant," said Bryce.

Harry Giles came in again, looking wary, and seemed even more disorientated than before. He sat down as directed.

"Now, Mr Giles, why did you come into the office late last night?" Bryce shot the question without preamble.

Harry looked even more flustered, and started to deny coming in at all.

"Oh, come on, Mr Giles – you were seen," said Bryce, conveniently ignoring the lack of positive identification from the only witness.

Harry writhed around in his chair for a few seconds, and then said "All right, so what if I did? I'm allowed to come in at any time."

Without answering, Bryce shot another question.

"You thought Neil Hazel was doing the coffee duty yesterday, didn't you?"

Harry half stood up, but Bryce snapped "sit

down" very sharply, and he collapsed back onto the chair and lowered his head onto his hands.

Eventually he said "I only know when it's my turn."

'Rubbish," responded Bryce.

"Must have been a shock for you to learn that Mr Kemp had been killed, wasn't it?" he continued.

Harry looked as though he would start to cry. "I didn't…" he broke off.

Bryce gave him no time to continue. He took another gamble.

"When you came in late on Monday night, I suppose you thought you weren't seen then either?"

"Oh God, I was so stupid," cried Harry, now with his head between his knees, his tears falling freely.

"What did Mr Hazel do to you?" asked Bryce, making yet another assumption without really having any evidence.

The ad man groaned. "He's always so nasty to Margaret, and pretty unpleasant all round. But I never intended him to die; I just wanted to give him a sharp shock.

"I checked the rota on Monday, but they must have done a swap without marking it up. I suppose I'll hang for this, but to my dying day I'll be constantly kicking myself for hurting poor John – he was a really good chap, as I told you before." Giles burst into tears.

"Harry Giles, I am arresting you on

suspicion of the murder of John Kemp," said Bryce. "You do not have to say anything, but anything you do say will be taken down and may be used in evidence.

"Jackson, I thought you'd come in handy. Handcuff him now, and take him to West End Central as it's nearest. Use your car. Sergeant Haig will come with you."

He took Haig aside.

"Get him booked in. I'll just speak to the others, and then come along myself. He's said enough before the three of us to charge him, but I'd just like to ask about how he knew about plugs, and get him to confirm that he set this up on Monday night. Then I'll charge him with the murder of Kemp."

Haig and Jackson left with Giles, and Bryce followed them into the outer office. Nobody spoke as the trio went out. Bryce sat on John Kemp's desk, which happened to be nearest. The five remaining people looked at him expectantly.

"Lady and gentlemen, I really don't need to say much. As you can see, Harry Giles has been arrested and will shortly be charged with murder. It may now be obvious to you all that poor Mr Kemp was not the intended victim. It was you, Mr Hazel, for reasons which will no doubt be aired in court."

Neil looked down at his desk, and said nothing.

"Giles says that he didn't intend for you to

die," the DCI continued. "That may well be true, but he was incredibly reckless. He was reckless in other ways too. For example, it's pure luck that neither Mr Hunter or Mr Lawn were injured or killed after Mr Lawn repaired the fuse.

"Anyway, I'll send someone round in the next day or two to take formal statements from all of you.

"There will be a trial in due course. It would be very unusual to get a guilty plea when the charge carries the death penalty. However, I anticipate there will be arguments about Giles' intention to kill, or perhaps even about his fitness to plead. In any case I shall be surprised if any of you actually have to give evidence. However, it's likely that some of you may have to give evidence at the inquest."

Mr Webb looked around at his remaining staff.

"I'm sure I speak for all of us, Chief Inspector, when I say how impressed – and grateful – we are that you've solved this so quickly. Can you tell us how you did it?"

Bryce smiled. "The only thing I can say – because this will come out in court anyway – is that your excellent cleaning lady provided a small but crucial piece of evidence. But please don't question her about it!"

Bryce took his leave of the subdued little office and drove the five hundred yards to the police station. The custody sergeant, who knew him from previous cases, greeted him with:

"Your boys are with him in the interview room, sir – he's singing like the proverbial canary!

"Even while we were booking him in, he was insisting on writing out a statement immediately. He said 'I'll dictate, you write'. Sergeant Haig asked him if he wanted a solicitor, and he turned him down. Would you care for a cup of tea, sir?"

Bryce gratefully accepted the offer. He decided not to join the others in the interview room – if Giles was talking, it was better not to interrupt his flow. Instead, when a constable brought his tea, he just leaned against the counter and chatted to the Sergeant about the traffic congestion in the city.

He had just finished his tea when Haig emerged from the interview room, with a smile from ear to ear.

"In the bag, sir – written down and signed. He shows no regret over trying to electrocute Hazel, but is genuinely devastated about Kemp.

Haig handed Bryce two sheets of paper, which the DCI scanned quickly.

"Well done, Sergeant. That certainly covers all the salient points."

"Do you think he'll get away with insanity, M'Naghten Rules and so on, sir," asked Haig.

"No, I don't. First, those Rules make it clear that a jury must assume everybody to be sane unless proved otherwise. His counsel would have to prove that he didn't know the 'nature and quality' of his action. Or, if he did know, that he didn't know it was wrong.

"From what we heard from him, he deliberately set out to harm Hazel. The rewiring of the plug shows that he knew what he was doing. And I can't see even the ablest KC trying to argue that his client didn't know it was wrong. After all, if Giles genuinely thought it was okay, he wouldn't have needed to creep into the office surreptitiously to set it up late at night.

"Nor do I think it matters whether or not he intended to kill. He admitted intending to cause harm – 'malice aforethought'. I'm rusty on my law, but in my book if death results from such an action, that's murder."

"Took a bit of a risk, didn't you sir, pretending we had evidence that he'd been identified coming into the office?"

"It was a gamble, admittedly. But I decided that bluff was the only way of getting him to confess. To be frank, if he hadn't 'coughed it', I don't know how we'd ever have proved which one of them did it.

"Anyway, come along and see if he says anything else when I formally charge him with murder."

DEATH IN THE PUBLIC BATHS

PETER ZANDER-HOWELL

Thursday 1ˢᵗ September 1949

Jack Carlo, Superintendent of the Seymour Place Public Baths, believed himself to be a lucky man. That being his conviction, and having by nature a grateful disposition, he began each day by counting his blessings.

He had survived the war with only minor injuries and was able to return to his old position at the baths. He had a healthy and hardworking wife in Pearl, and a fine son in Victor. His steady employment at the baths was in no way unpleasant, and it gave them all a fair living.

Whichever way Jack arranged his daily count, his list always included the benefit of their three-bedroom flat, provided by the St Marylebone Borough Council so that he could live on the premises.

He realised it was a mutual benefit; in giving him the flat the Council had a twenty-four-hour guardian at the baths. But Jack, who had grown up in two rooms of a Heneage Street tenement in London's East End, thought he would never take for granted such well-appointed spaciousness. Five of them had lived in those two rooms when he was a lad. No bathroom. The single privy was shared with everyone else in the building. Now, he and his little family had not only three bedrooms, but two living rooms, a kitchen, and a bathroom. Jack was pleased that negotiating a communal staircase to slop out a bucket in the mornings would never be part of Victor's boyhood.

His counting complete, the Superintendent turned out of bed at five past six as usual. A thorough wash and double-quick dressing found him at the door and ready to leave fifteen minutes later, clipboard and pencil in hand. Pearl, just getting out of bed and hearing the door being opened, called out to him as she always did:

"Breakfast at seven, Jack."

An unnecessary reminder, as their timetable never varied; but it was another little thread of predictability in his post-war life, and he welcomed it.

****

When the Public Baths opened in 1937 it was clear that the Council had created a remarkable building. In common with similar council establishments up and down the country, its purpose was to improve the hygiene and health of the local population. This was achieved in a variety of ways in different parts of the building, the one common factor being the supply of water.

Twelve years and one war later, little had changed at the baths. Whatever slum clearance intentions the authorities may have had before the war, Seymour Place was still essential for occupants of all the inadequate dwellings which had withstood the Luftwaffe's calling cards.

That morning, Jack was doing a 'whisk-through': spot-checking the order and cleanliness of the facilities. This was always best done when the building was completely empty and he could move around freely, without engaging in conversations with staff and customers. Not that the Superintendent didn't have time for such chats – on the contrary, he considered those interactions to be an integral part of his role, and always made himself available. But the early morning walks gave him a different perspective of his domain, and he could accomplish a lot more uninterrupted.

As usual, he first went at a brisk pace around the slipper baths, checking all fifty of them. The baths were cleaned out after each user by a little team led by Florrie Machin, one of his most conscientious members of staff. As expected, there was nothing for him to take issue with in the bathrooms. He would have been pleased to take a soak in any of the tubs himself and, when he came back later in the day, he would tell Florrie so.

In the laundry room, apart from one slowly dripping tap which had already been reported by the head attendant, the twenty-five laundry troughs were as they should be, and the room was otherwise silent. That silence would quickly change into a noisy hubbub as soon as the laundry opened. Old prams would start arriving, and balanced on these would be huge bundles of dirty washing, gathered together in bed sheets. With the bundles would come the voices of the women who pushed the prams, gossiping, laughing, and exchanging household tips over the soap bubbles in their troughs.

Norman Potts, in charge of this section, boasted he had the best job in the baths. There was almost never a need for him to sort out a squabble, and only once had he been required to separate a pair of viragos. (An unfortunate episode; two women laying claim to the affections of the same man and passing loud and spiteful judgement on each other's morals.) Instead, his days were mostly spent joining in with the lively banter as he patrolled the various rooms that made up the laundry, mopped up spills, and enjoyed the affectionate 'old Potty' jokes he knew were made about him as soon as his back was turned.

Passing through the laundry, Jack saw that the mangle, drying and ironing areas were also of a satisfactory standard, but he made a note that the pram store needed a better going-over.

The small swimming pool was next for his attention. This was a shallow pool, some 100 feet long and 30 feet wide, ideal for learners and fledgling swimmers gaining confidence. Jack checked the water, and saw that nothing needed to be done. The changing rooms, together with the towel store and its issuing counter, also passed muster; as did the area behind the counter.

The large swimming pool was last on Jack's route before he checked the Bryanston Place admissions booth, after which he would make his way to other parts of the complex.

This pool was an impressive 132 feet long and 42 feet wide, equipped with a diving board. There were 450 seats for spectators, arranged in rows of stepped tiers along one length of the pool. The entire area was, by design, multi-purpose. When the pool was drained – to show a film, or stage a theatre production – up to another 1400 people could be seated.

The roof – if such a mundane description could be applied to an almost cathedral-like structure – was barrel-vaulted, with tiered vertical windows between the curving concrete beams. Without question, this was Jack's favourite part of the baths, and he paused to enjoy it before climbing the steps to the spectator seats.

Walking between the two central rows, he quickly checked the rows above and below for overlooked litter and lost property. Pleased to find that there was nothing for him to collect, he descended the steps at the far end and made his way towards the Bryanston Place entrance – where he suddenly stopped short. Astounded by what he saw, he muttered out loud:

"I know I bolted this door top and bottom last night. Absolutely sure I did. No two ways about it."

The building was still secure, but the door should not have been unbolted. There was nothing he could do apart from shake his head in bewilderment at the fact.

Perplexed, the Superintendent slowly made his way towards the large pool again, this time aiming to walk back around the side opposite the spectator seats, so that he could inspect that area and beyond.

In taking this approach he immediately saw what he had missed when walking the other way: in the shadow at the side of the pool was a body, floating face down and partly submerged.

Rejecting the idea that kicking off his shoes and swimming across the pool would get him to the motionless figure fastest, Jack ran around the perimeter instead. Kneeling at the spot, he saw the body was dressed in jacket, trousers, and shoes, and assessed it to be a man. There was nothing to be done for him.

Up on his feet again, Jack didn't waste a second. Looking at the pool clock he realised that the two senior admission clerks would by now be waiting to come in at the Shouldham Street door. Bertha Morland and Alf Sharp always made an early start each day; Alf ran the Shouldham entrance booth, and Bertha the Bryanston entrance one.

Unbolting and then unlocking the Shouldham door to the pair, Jack gave them a quick explanation. Both asked if there was anything they could do, and to both he answered:

"No; just you stay put for the moment. We shall likely need to deal with the public at some point, but right now, anyone who turns up will have to wait outside for a bit, until I've had a chance to call the old bill."

"What about some notices for the doors, Jack? Should we put something up sooner rather than later this time?" asked Bertha. "Perhaps telling people to come back this afternoon? Otherwise we'll have scores of unhappy customers queuing around the block, with no idea for how long."

"Yes," agreed Alf. "And we should do a notice that staff using Bertha's door are to come round to Shouldham instead. All of them can wait in here with me, well away from that end of the building."

The Superintendent agreed that temporary closure notices were for the best, and authorised the clerks to make suitable signs. And Bertha was right; it wasn't an unheard-of occurrence to close the building for a while. In the past he had dealt with both electrical and water supply failures which had necessitated just such action.

Leaving the clerks, he ran up to the flat to give an explanation to Pearl, warning her not to take the shortcut through the large pool when taking Victor to school, and instead to use their private exit onto Shouldham Street.

"If people are waiting to come in by that entrance when you leave, you'll have to say the baths are closed for the moment without saying why," he told her. "Bertha and Alf are putting up notices, but people may still try and pester you. We'll have to wait 'til the body's removed before we can get going again."

Pearl's eyes had grown round in astonishment as she listened to her husband's account of his discovery, but her manner was calm. She knew that accidents happened in public baths; inevitable, really, when you thought about the environment. So far, however, there had been nothing other than the most minor incidents during her husband's tenure. Pearl unhappily realised that a fully-dressed drowning would be an exceptional occurrence in any council pool, and would definitely call into question Jack's procedures at the baths. She was extremely sorry that her husband's good safety record had been broken in this way.

"Do you know who it is?" she asked.

"No – well, I've not seen his face yet, so I suppose I may recognise him. I'm telephoning for the police next, and we'll have to see what happens after that. I'll get back for my bit of breakfast whenever I can."

Reassured that his fried bread and bacon was already covered with a plate and on a low light in the oven, he gave his wife's cheek a quick peck and made his way to his office.

Dialling 999, Carlo told the operator that he needed police and an ambulance. Once connected, he reported the accidental drowning, explained that he had no idea of the man's identity, and requested prompt assistance so that the facility could be operational again as soon as possible. He hung up the telephone and immediately went back to the Bryanston Place door to wait for help.

****

The ambulance arrived very quickly. Before the two crewmen had time to unload a stretcher from the back of the vehicle a fresh-faced constable came swooping around the corner on a bicycle. Spotting the bloodwagon halfway down the road, the officer swung a leg over his bike frame and coasted along to the door, balancing with a foot on one pedal, ready for a rapid stop. As he dismounted, the older of the ambulance men greeted Jack with a cheery:

"'Mornin' guvnor. Someone's gone and

drownded hisself for you, then?"

Rather less cheerily, Jack confirmed that was the case. Letting the three men into the building, he bolted the door behind them and led the way through to the large pool.

"Nothing I could do for him when I found him, and I couldn't have got him out by myself," explained the Superintendent as the four men looked down at the deceased.

Turning to a nearby wall, Jack took down a long pole which was hanging beside a life ring and some floats. A couple of unsuccessful attempts were made before he succeeded in hooking the canvas loop at the end of the pole around the man's shoulders. Walking the body along to the shallow end, the ambulance men helped him to drag it from the water.

Rolling the man onto his back, the ambulance man nearest the head let out a loud "Cor blimey!"

As he drew back, the others could see what had surprised him: in the centre of the dead man's forehead was a ragged hole. It was now abundantly clear to the four that this was not a case of accidental drowning.

Jack realised, despite the head damage he did in fact recognise the man, and vaguely thought he may have heard someone else call him Jimmy.

The Constable coughed. He had seen a handful of dead bodies before, but as yet, no-one who had been murdered. Training took over,

"Righty-ho," he said. "You three better stand back and keep well away from that. I shall have to call the station."

Realising that he was very much in charge until help showed up, the young PC turned to Jack,

"You, sir – what's your name?"

Jack gave his details. The Constable wrote in his pocketbook and then spent a minute or so thinking whilst the others waited silently. Finally clear in his mind on the best way forward, he said to the ambulance team:

"Don't see much point you two hanging about. I reckon this here won't be moved for hours yet."

To the Superintendent he said:

"If you let the ambulance crew out, Mr Carlo, and then show me to your telephone, that'd be grand. Have you stopped anyone else getting in?"

Jack confirmed that the doors were both secured, and that other than his family the two clerks were the only staff in the building. He added that by this time he expected the clerks to have displayed notices at both entrances advising a temporary closure.

Directing the Constable to his office, he next escorted the two ambulance men out of the building and fastened the Bryanston Place door behind them again, returning to his office just as the policeman was hanging up the receiver.

"Our Divisional Detective Inspector says he's calling in the Yard straight away. That means the brass are coming, Mr Carlo. The police surgeon too, I daresay. We'd better just wait by the entrance door for them."

Stationed by the door again, Jack pointed out the two large bolts to the Constable,

"Last night, I pushed those home myself. First the top and then the bottom. Slipped them all the way along – and turned the knobs into their slots. Secure as you like; same as I always do. But this morning I come down and find them both undone."

Jack also suggested the possible name of Jimmy for the man, but stressed it was just an inkling rather than any definite knowledge.

The officer made his notes, and whilst he was occupied Jack tried to work out how and when the man had died. Presently he asked the Constable his opinion:

"What do you reckon made that hole then?"

"Well, either someone's smashed him in the head with a drill bit or similar, or else that was a bullet coming out. I've read that a bullet can make a lot more mess coming out that it does going in."

"Yes, now you mention it I've seen a case in the army myself. I suppose we didn't see the entry point at the back because it was covered by his hair?"

"Likely, yes," replied the constable.

Leaving the policeman to watch the door, Jack went to speak to his wife before she set off for school with Victor.

By the time he reached the flat, Pearl and Victor were already in the hallway. Not wanting his son to hear, Jack bent down to the boy, put a hand on his cheek and did something he had never done before – told him a lie:

"Your Auntie Bertha and Uncle Alf want to see your new drawing, son; that beauty you did with your new colours."

"The rag and bone man's horse d'you mean, Daddy?"

"That's the one. Fetch it from your room, will you?"

With the boy safely out of earshot, Jack quickly explained the latest development to Pearl.

Pearl's response on hearing about the gun wound and Scotland Yard's involvement was a steady "Well I never did, Jack," accompanied by an affectionate squeezing and patting of his arm.

As unflustered as her voice and actions were, Pearl's thoughts were churning. She now felt a flicker of hope that, when the time came to face questions from the Council, the violent and criminal manner of the man's arrival in the pool must surely help Jack.

All of this would need discussing with him, of course, but this was not the time for such a conversation. Pearl determined that whilst her husband was dealing with the immediate aspects of the situation, she would make it her job to think about how he might best meet his employer's inquiry when it came.

"Did you recognise him, Jack, once he was turned over and you could get a good look?" she asked.

"Yes. I've definitely seen him around and about before, and I'm thinking his name might be Jimmy. Don't suppose that would mean anything to you, pet?"

His wife shook her head. It was a common enough name, but the only Jimmy she knew was six years old and one of Victor's classmates.

Jack's stomach rumbled loudly. He was tempted to delay going back and put himself on the outside of his fried bread and bacon first. But he thought better of it. The ambulance and bobby had both arrived very quickly indeed; he didn't want to be absent when Scotland Yard arrived, and have them think he wasn't taking matters seriously.

With another quick peck for Pearl's cheek, the Superintendent was just letting himself out when from behind him a little voice called:

"Here's my picture, Daddy."

****

Within ten minutes of Jack rejoining the police officer there was a banging on the metal Art Deco door. Two men in civilian clothing were waiting to be admitted. The taller man turned to Jack and opened the introductions:

"Detective Chief Inspector Bryce of Scotland

Yard, and this is Detective Sergeant Haig. I gather you've woken up to trouble here today?"

Jack supplied his name and brief details of his responsibilities; how he had first discovered the deceased; and how he had waited for the police and ambulance to arrive before moving the man and bringing him out of the water.

Thanking the Superintendent, Bryce turned to the uniformed officer. Chin pulled in and chest pushed out, the young man stood to attention like a statue, barely moving his lips to identify himself as:

"Constable Stanton, sir."

The Chief Inspector glanced around the entrance area before turning to the Superintendent:

"Stay here please, Mr Carlo, let the doctor in when he arrives and bring him along to join us. He'll be here within quarter of an hour. In the meantime, you lead on, Stanton, first to the exact spot where the Superintendent showed you the body."

The three policemen went through to the large pool. Unlike Sergeant Haig (who had once brought his daughter to the swimming pool as a change from their local baths) Bryce had never visited the building. He had, however, read about the beautiful design of the roof and windows. After inspecting the section of pool Stanton identified as the original location of the body, he took a moment to admire the structure above, at the same time appreciating the unusual amount of natural light illuminating the crime scene for him.

Reaching the victim, Bryce hitched up his trousers at the knee and squatted.

"I don't recognise him, sir, do you?" Sergeant Haig asked as he busied himself with his camera.

"No, I'm pretty sure I've never seen him before. What about you, Stanton?"

"No, sir, I don't know him, but I've only been in this Division a few weeks so it's possible he's got a reputation here that I haven't heard about. All I can tell you is Mr Carlo reports that he found that outside door we all came through unbolted this morning. He also says the dead man was a regular here, and thinks his name might be 'Jimmy'."

"Hmm, it's not much to go on but it's all useful; good," said the DCI, pleased to have even the smallest scraps of information with which to start his investigation. To Haig he said:

"When you're done taking all the photographs, go through his pockets, Sergeant. We'll wait for the doctor before turning him over again, but from the exit wound I think we'll find a heavy calibre entry wound at the base of the skull – I'd guess a point four five."

Bryce stood up and quickly considered his options before turning to Stanton,

"Have you worked with detectives before, Constable?"

"No, sir. I've not had the chance to work with plain clothes."

"No matter. We'll borrow you for a bit all the same," replied Bryce, deciding that utilising the uniformed officer on hand was preferable to calling for a detective constable who might take some time to appear. "I'll share my thinking out loud, and you'll get a bit of detective experience."

A beaming smile from the local man told Bryce that his decision was acceptable.

"We'll assume for the moment the victim was killed there," said the DCI, pointing to the section of pool where Stanton had first shown the body was discovered and which Sergeant Haig was now photographing.

"Apart from the fact that there's no trail of blood anywhere, in this situation I can't think of a reason why the assailant would drag a dead man around the building. So the assumption that the shot was fired over there, and the victim fell in at the same point, is logical. What logical assumption can you make from this exit wound, Officer?"

Taken completely by surprise, the Constable swung his eyes away from the farther end of the pool and back down to the body at Bryce's feet. His mind was a perfect blank. He thought he would have to confess to the Yard Inspector that nothing at all occurred to him – logical or otherwise.

However, not wanting to admit to a void in his own head before he absolutely had to, he repeated Bryce's question out loud "What logical assumption can I make from the exit wound, sir?" and suddenly found himself focusing on the operative word: 'exit'.

"We need to hunt for the bullet?" he suggested, his voice and face both showing relief that he was able to demonstrate the expected logical thought. "It has to be somewhere hereabouts, doesn't it, sir, because it's not in his head?"

"Correct. We've got no idea which way the victim was facing when he was shot, which means we have no idea of trajectory. We need to systematically search this entire area – until we meet a solid obstruction in every direction. Go round the pool, close to the edge, on your hands and knees looking into the water – it's quite still and clear – and see if you can spot a bullet. If not, look all around the pool, especially in corners. You can look for a shell case too. But, if this is a professional killing and the gunman used an automatic which ejected the shell case, I'd expect him to tidy up after himself and pick it up."

"Very good, sir," replied the Constable, realising that he was part of something extraordinary – a gangland murder – if the Chief Inspector was correct.

Sergeant Haig had just finished his search of the man's pockets. He deposited a small collection of coins, keys, wallet and documents onto a dry area of floor.

"There's a ration book, and an ID card in the wallet amongst that little lot, sir, but all soaked through, of course. Perhaps best let everything dry out a wee bit before trying to examine it?"

"Yes. Leave it all there for the moment, and help Stanton look for the bullet, and perhaps there may be a shell case too. It'd be too much to hope for to find the gun, but I'm always open to being pleasantly surprised, Sergeant!"

At this point Jack returned, his second cheerful visitor of the morning following close behind. This was the police surgeon; short and balding, on the right side of forty, and breezily swinging a medical bag as he strode along.

"Good morning to you, Philip!" boomed the doctor, his naturally loud voice amplified by the water and tiled surfaces of the pool. Gazing up at the roof, the medic added "I appreciate these are brighter and more salubrious surroundings than others you've dragged me out to recently, old chap, but it would still be rather nice to see you one day without a dead body between us!"

"Good morning to you as well, Paul," said Bryce, "and if you're kept as busy as I am you can't have time for a social life," he retorted with a smile.

The police surgeon knelt beside the body and conducted a few basic tests. Asking Bryce to help him roll the man over, he gently parted the thick, wet black hair, and said:

"Well, as you've no doubt surmised, he was shot from behind. I'll be able to see better when I can get him on the slab and shave the hair away, but the exit wound suggests a heavy bullet – at least a point three eight, but almost certainly a point four five." He waved towards Haig and Stanton who, from opposite directions, had inched their way round to the other side of the pool and were now only a few feet away from converging, "I assume that's what they're looking for?"

Bryce nodded.

"Again, I need to do more tests, and it doesn't help that the man's been immersed in cold water, but provisionally I'd say he's been dead for at least eight hours. If you work on the basis that he was killed between ten o'clock and midnight yesterday, you'll be in the right timeframe. If you're happy he's moved, I'll arrange to get him along to St Mary's as soon as possible."

"Yes, go ahead," confirmed Bryce. "Haig has taken all the photographs we need, and if we can't find the bullet we shall be finished in here very soon ourselves."

Farewells given, and with Jack acting as escort again, Dr Bates departed.

The DCI now gave his attention to the heap of sodden items his Sergeant had collected. He was just debating whether to attempt to remove the ID card from the wallet when the Superintendent returned. Not realising that the Constable had already passed on the information, Jack wanted to report the unbolted door.

"Yes, thank you Mr Carlo. I'm guessing this is a professional job, so the chances of fingerprints are zero, but we'll dust the door anyway," said Bryce.

"The door wasn't the only strange happening, sir. About fifteen minutes after locking up last night, I was having a cup of cocoa when I heard a noise – a loud crashing sound. Crossed my mind that one of the big windows in here had fallen in, because I couldn't think what else in the building might make that sort of crashing noise."

Jack paused, and Bryce could see that he was hesitating about saying more. He was just about to encourage the Superintendent to continue by reminding him that withholding information was a serious matter, when Jack spoke again:

"It was about quarter to eleven, sir, and I'll tell you straight that I didn't hurry myself to check when perhaps I should have. But my reasoning was that no-one could possibly be hurt by a falling window when the building was empty; and no-one would come to do a repair before morning, either. So, no, I didn't rush myself and now," Jack looked unhappily at the body, "with him like that, poor chap, I regret it.

"When I'd finished my cocoa, I did nip down for a look at the windows, just to see what was what." The superintendent shrugged and shook his head, "Well, nothing to see with the windows. I went back to my flat and to bed soon after."

"Quarter to eleven, you say," Bryce nodded thoughtfully, "I think we can assume you heard the shot. A large calibre pistol makes a loud enough bang; firing it inside this huge hall might make it sound quite unlike a gunshot – and much louder.

"And if that was what you heard, Mr Carlo, you needn't regret not coming down immediately; the gunman might have shot you too!

"Incidentally, who was the woman we saw in the booth by the entrance when we arrived?" asked the DCI.

Jack explained about Bertha and Alf.

"I see." said Bryce. He thought for a moment. "I was about to say that you could send those two home and close down for the rest of the day. However, I'm pretty sure now that the shot was fired in here, so although we will need look elsewhere, we can leave that for a bit.

"Right now, Mr Carlo, I need to understand how the victim was able to be in the building last night. You said you close at half past ten. Do you go into every single room to check that everyone has left?"

This was the question Jack was dreading. He couldn't see any way of giving his reply without sounding at best slack and at worst incompetent – neither of which were even half true.

"No, I don't go into every single room. This is a large complex, and each member of staff will check their own area – some being easier to check than others. There's an electric bell which is loud and can be heard everywhere. That sounds fifteen minutes before we close, and again five minutes before. Everyone knows what that means."

"So presumably someone could hide in one of the rooms, and come out after you'd locked up?" queried Bryce.

Jack didn't need to deliberate at all before replying:

"Yes, dozens of places. There are the slipper baths – fifty of them, for starters. The laundry room – troughs and washing machines area; mangling, drying, and ironing rooms; pram store, lavatories, café with kitchen and scullery, my office, the filtration room, storerooms – plenty of those dotted all over the place. Pool changing rooms; and dressing rooms for when this hall is used for performances..."

Bryce held up his hand, "I get the picture, thank you. What you're saying is that someone could hide in the building after time and realistically nobody would know."

"Exactly, sir," replied Jack. "To a certain extent we have to rely on people leaving when they're meant to. And before this happened, they did!" He paused a moment before asking, "But when you say 'someone', surely this situation must mean that two people hid – the dead man and whoever did for him?"

"That would seem to be so, Mr Carlo, and at some point I shall need a statement about everything you've told me, but we can sort that out later.

"The body will be removed shortly. Then,

if we can find the bullet, I don't see why you shouldn't open everything up again when you're ready – or do you have to drain and refill the pool now?"

"I'll ring the Council and take advice on that; see what the Health Officer says, but I should think not. There's filters and chemicals and things, and anyway, there was hardly any blood as far as I can see. It'd take days to drain and refill it."

"Is it okay if I go and see my wife in the flat now, Mr Bryce? I was just going to get my breakfast when I found the dead man."

"Yes, you do that; but first tell your clerk at the Bryanston door to be ready to let the ambulance people in when they arrive," replied the DCI

Jack went off to give the instruction just as Haig gave a shout from the far corner of the huge hall:

"Got it, sir!"

The Sergeant came back to the DCI, carrying a somewhat deformed bullet on his open notebook.

"Stanton is still looking for a shell case sir."

"Excellent," said Bryce, peering at the bullet. "A point four five for sure. That's as far as the good news goes, unfortunately. Only a million or two guns made which could fire that – so not much chance of finding the right one."

"Bottom of the Thames by now, would you say, sir?" asked Haig.

"Possibly. Still, if we can't get any further with the gun we have other avenues to pursue. I'm not sure what state his fingers will be in, Sergeant, but see what you can get in the way of prints. Keep Stanton looking for a shell case."

A visibly weary and still breakfast-less Superintendent re-appeared, this time with two new stretcher-bearing ambulance men in tow.

"At the door just as I got there," said Jack.

Bryce addressed the new arrivals:

"The Sergeant will finish fingerprinting in a minute. Then you can load the victim up and get him to St Mary's for Doctor Bates to do the PM as soon as possible."

To the waiting Superintendent he said:

"You go, Mr Carlo. We'll deal with everything here; and when we're done your clerk at the door can see us out. By the time you get back we'll hopefully be long gone."

Jack left the poolside and finally disappeared.

The DCI called to the local officer:

"Give up the search, Stanton. If it was a revolver, there's nothing to find, and if it was an automatic any self-respecting killer will have picked up the shell case anyway. Thank you; you've been a good help. When you've seen the body into the ambulance, you can get back to your normal duties." To Haig he said:

"Sergeant, take your gear and dust the main door for prints. Fruitless, perhaps, but we must try.

While you're doing that, I'll bag up the victim's pocket contents – we'll check those out back at the Yard." Bryce scanned the pool in all directions, "I was intending to look in every room before we left. But looking at the size of what I can see from here, and having heard Carlo's list, it'd take all week and won't be the best use of our time."

****

Sergeant Haig took the wheel for the journey back to Scotland Yard. As the Wolseley passed down Park Lane, the DCI began to muse out loud:

"I wonder if you're right about the gun being in the Thames. The murderer could have chucked it in the pool, but didn't. That makes some sense, of course; he's used it once on the victim, but he may have wanted to keep it a bit longer as insurance, just in case someone tried to apprehend him either inside the building, or as he left. But nobody would keep it any longer than he had to."

"Except the idiots who shot PC Gutteridge back in 1927", interposed Haig. "They'd never have hanged if one of them hadnae kept the pistol."

"True, but we should expect that every gun-toting criminal must have learned from that case. Anyway, we know our assailant left by the Bryanston Place door. Theorising that he would have dumped the gun as soon as possible I think, on balance, it's worth a search in the vicinity. Only a small chance, but again, we have to try.

"As soon as we get to the Yard, arrange for

a team of four men with DC Kittow in charge. Use only our people, not 'D' Division men. When the Marylebone Inspector asked us to take this case, he said he was swamped. No doubt he's experiencing the same staff shortages that other forces are.

"Anyway, get them to go through every bin they can find within, say, fifty yards of that door. That'll take them into Shouldham Street and Seymour Place too. Equip them with suitable gloves. I don't care if they leave a bit of mess; if the gun is in a bin I want it found, and quickly. Remind them that the chances are there will still be live rounds in it."

Bryce invited his Sergeant's thoughts now:

"How do you think we should tackle the investigation with what we have so far, Haig?"

Alex Haig was pleased to be asked. He had worked for senior detectives who had never sought an opinion or any real involvement from him, operating a 'jump to it, and no questions' system of policing.

"I think we should work on the theory that the two knew each other, sir, and follow up all leads to their connection in the pocket contents. Always keeping in mind that the papers in his pockets aren't the victim's and may be forgeries. Or genuine papers – but not his; put in his pockets to throw us off the trail."

"Agreed," said Bryce, smiling with quiet satisfaction at the confident way in which his Sergeant was expressing his thoughts and thinking through the possibilities. He felt sure Haig would be a good candidate for inspector in a few more years.

"And, for the moment, we have to assume that before closing time the gunman somehow persuaded his victim to stay in the building – perhaps at gunpoint – until he was ready to shoot him. You're absolutely right that we need those leads, and while you're sorting out a gun searching party, I'll make a start with the documents he had on him.

"Once you've got the search underway, Haig, go down to the fingerprint department and see if you can find a match with the ones you took off the victim.

"Finally, get those pictures developed. And ask the photographic people to somehow blank out the hole in his head and print a facial shot that doesn't look too awful. It will take a few hours to do, I don't doubt, but showing a decent photo around will still be the quickest way for us to check if the clerks or other staff remembers the victim arriving yesterday. If someone does remember, there's a chance they might also recall if he was with another man they recognise."

Haig acknowledged his instructions as they pulled into the Yard and the two detectives went their separate ways.

****

Arriving at his fourth-floor office, Bryce

stopped first at his secretary's desk and asked for two sheets of clean blotting paper.

Next, he took off his jacket and slipped it onto the hanger on the coat stand by the door before clearing a space on a small table at the side of his office and hitching up his sleeves.

He spread out one sheet of blotting paper and eased out the documents from the envelope in which they had been carried. The second sheet of blotting paper was gently pressed over the little heap and the items separated.

The ration book was in a sorry condition. The identity card, however, somewhat protected in its small leather wallet, was the better preserved of the two documents even though black leather dye had soaked into it. Bryce focused his attention on this and slowly carried on pressing the absorbent paper against it.

When the card had been blotted sufficiently for his purposes, he very carefully introduced the point of a slender letter opener between the compressed folds of card at one corner, before cautiously peeling the two halves apart.

A smile spread across his face. Miraculously, the card was legible. It had been issued in 1939 to a James Green; age 36. The address was recorded as 87 Ranston Street; and Green's occupation as 'Railway Fireman'.

Picking up the telephone, he called the fingerprint department.

"DCI Bryce here," he announced. "Has

Sergeant Haig arrived? Good. Put him on the line, please.

"I don't know how far you've got, Sergeant, but we have a name from the ID card – James Green. That tallies with the Superintendent's feeling his name was Jimmy, so the documents probably do match the man. Dig about whilst you're down there and see if we have anything on him. Then come back up here."

****

Sergeant Haig was knocking on the DCI's door twenty minutes later.

"That was quick, Haig. You've obviously made progress"

"Aye, I have, sir. We have fingerprint records and a mugshot for Green. He was sent down in 1944 for an offence under the Forgery Act – dodgy pound notes. He got three years for 'uttering'. He's been out for a year or so." Haig passed some index cards across the desk to his boss.

"Good work," said Bryce. He looked at the mugshot, taken when Green was arrested. Satisfied with it, he unclipped the photograph from its card and passed it to Haig.

"Two more jobs for you. Now we have this mugshot there's no need to wait for the photographic department to make us a special photo. Pity we have only the one, though. It would have speeded things up to have a second photo – then two of you could go back to the baths.

Anyway, you go and show it around to all the staff; ticket clerks, pool attendants – absolutely anyone and everyone – until you hear something helpful about Green's visit yesterday.

"When you've done that, pick up a DC and go along to 87 Ranston Street – that was the address on his ID card and his Ration Book. Find out if there's a wife or anyone else living there.

"He was carrying his ration book, which suggests he did his own food shopping, so I rather doubt he was married. But if you do find someone connected with him there, I leave it to you to ask all the necessary questions about enemies and so forth. Oh, and take his keys from the table over there, and see if they fit any of his doors. Let yourself in if no-one's home.

"Whilst you're doing all of that, I'm going to call up the full file on Green and see if it will shed any more light for us."

"Aye, all understood, sir," replied Haig, tucking his notebook and pencil into his jacket pocket before leaving to carry out his orders.

****

Bryce picked up his telephone to call the Records Department.

"Sergeant Gilbert? DCI Bryce here. I'm after a file for a James Green. Yes, both common names, unfortunately. Yes, I imagine you will have a few of them. Yes, I know you're very busy. The one I want is a Green with only two 'e's – no third 'e' on the end. Convicted at the Old Bailey on September 5th, 1944. Given three years for uttering. It's in connection with a murder so I need the file up here quick as you can. Do your best for me, please, Sergeant."

Receiver replaced, Bryce was satisfied that he had a promising avenue of investigation opening up before him, but at the same time wondered if he was wasting a lot of police time with the bin search. Manpower was generally in short supply, with forces up and down the country depleted and coping with significant recruitment and retention problems. He also wondered if he should have gone to Green's address, rather than sending Haig, but reminded himself that his Sergeant needed independence, and room to prove himself as good inspector material.

A knocking on his door disrupted the DCI's thoughts. Looking up, he was astonished to see the Records Officer arrive in the room bearing a well-filled folder and wearing a huge 'who's-a-clever-boy' smirk across his face.

"Green's file, sir."

Bryce gave him a wry smile and drily enquired:

"The first file you pulled out, then, Gilbert?

"Yes, sir. Just happens lucky like that sometimes."

Bryce thanked the Sergeant and opened the folder. He started with the most recent entries first, and in less than five minutes looked up from his reading. For the second time in quick succession, he called Records. The Sergeant had only just got back to his desk.

"Apologies Gilbert, but can you find me everything you have on a Leonard Attwater – convicted at the same time as James Green."

"I'll do my best for you, sir," promised the Records Sergeant.

Bryce had hardly put the telephone down when it rang again.

"DC Kittow here, sir," said the voice at the other end of the line.

"Kittow; have you found something?"

"Yes sir – an automatic pistol in a bin not thirty yards from the bath house door. Found it myself. What should I do with it, sir?"

"Bring it back to the Yard. Don't touch it more than you have to, of course. But if you know how to take out the bullet in the chamber – if there is one – I think you'd better do that. And extract the magazine as well.

"Tell the uniform chaps to report back to Inspector Rawlings. And Kittow – well done."

Bryce rubbed his hands in satisfaction. With matters bubbling along nicely in the case, and nothing more for him to do for the moment, he started to attack his 'in' tray. Reading the accumulation of correspondence was his priority task, followed by telephone calls which had been taken whilst he was out, and which he now had time to return.

****

Alex Haig made his way back to the baths and entered through the Bryanston Place door, where Bertha Morland was issuing tickets to a gaggle of boys. Signalling that he would wait until she had dealt with the little group, he stood against a nearby wall.

The boys quickly paid and passed through a turnstile until only one lad – who had noticeably hung behind his pals – was left. This boy was much smaller than his friends, and even more shabbily dressed. Tucked beneath a spindly arm he carried a roll of the most washed-out worn-out towelling that Haig had ever seen, presumably with some sort of bathing costume inside.

Arriving at Bertha's window, the child set down a collection of coins and said in a low voice:

"I'm three ha'pence short today, Missus."

Haig watched and listened. He was struck by how peely-wally the child looked, and the air of neediness about him. The thought that the cashier might turn the boy away from the pool for want of a penny ha'penny was unthinkable to him. Equally, he understood that making up shortfalls for customers was not something that a Council employee could – or should fund themselves. The Sergeant's hand was in his pocket immediately.

Before he could fish out and present the necessary coins, Bertha was leaning towards the boy. With a fearsome cast in her left eye and an unfortunate complexion, the cashier didn't make a very sympathetic impression. Haig was soon to learn, however, that finding a kinder woman than Bertha Morland would be a search that anyone who knew her wouldn't even bother to start.

"Well then, Arnie! You must have had a good week with the bottles, did you, if you're only three ha'pence short today?"

The boy nodded, and held his head a little a higher with the recognition of his success.

"I went with Steven and Petey. We took the pushcart to the streets behind the park, like you said. No one collects round that way. We went four days runnin' and got bottles ev'ry day. We got all the deposits back."

"Gave most of the money to your Mum, did you, Arnie?"

The boy nodded again.

Bertha quickly unlocked the drawer where she kept her handbag and other personal effects. From it she took a ha'penny and four farthings to make up the child's entrance fee, and swept his coins and hers into the cash drawer and shut it.

Next, she pushed some extra coins towards him, her hand over the top of them so that the Sergeant couldn't see how much, and said:

"You go with your big brothers to the eel shop and get some pie and mash tonight, before you go home."

Arnold put his small hand gently over the top of Bertha's; as she slid her hand away he took the money that was now beneath his own fingers. Haig was moved by how shyly and un-graspingly the child did this, even though he was certain this was not some new or unfamiliar arrangement between the boy and the cashier.

"Thank you ever so, Missus,"

"Catch your friends up in the pool now, Arnie, and I'll see you next week. That'll be after school though, won't it, with the holidays finished?"

The boy nodded. Giving Bertha the most radiant of smiles, he went through the turnstile. Haig stepped away from the wall.

"Is the wee laddie short every week?"

"Always. They have a very hard life, that family. Rationing's not much use if you haven't enough money to buy your quotas."

Bertha fussed with a few things at her window before adding:

"You'd be surprised how often the cleaners pick up bits and pieces of small change. Coppers mostly, with the odd thruppenny piece. No-one ever seems to miss it, or bothers to ask if it's been handed in. They bring it to me, and I keep it in my drawer – the girls know what I do with it."

All of this was perfectly true. But suggesting Arnie and his older brothers should get pie and mash – or a saveloy and chips for that matter – was always done entirely with her own money. Bertha felt no one else needed to know it.

"Do you want to talk to me about this

morning?" she asked, changing the subject.

Sergeant Haig showed Jimmy's picture and the cashier confirmed she recognised him, although she didn't know his name was Jimmy Green until told. She had never seen anyone else come in with him.

"He used to buy a washing machine ticket, once a fortnight or so. He never went swimming that I know of. Maybe he went to the café whilst his wash was going round. Worth your while having a word with the café staff next, I'd say, Sergeant."

Haig decided to act on that suggestion, and see if he could gather enough information from the café staff to save him showing the photo elsewhere at the baths.

Thanking the cashier, and ready to leave, he took his hand out of his pocket and put down all the change he had been carrying at Bertha's window, some sixpences shining amongst the coppers. As he turned away, he said with a smile:

"You'd think someone would have noticed they'd dropped that little lot by the wall."

****

Back at the Yard, Bryce had been ploughing through his paperwork without a break for more than two hours before he realised how much time had passed. Picking up the telephone, he decided to make a last call before going to find something to eat.

He was mid-conversation with his opposite

number in the Norfolk constabulary, discussing black market activity that was affecting their respective areas, when another knock on his door presaged the return of Sergeant Gilbert.

Tapping his watch and mouthing an apologetic 'sorry' at the DCI, the Records officer put the file on the desk and quietly withdrew again.

With the telephone receiver back in its cradle, the temptation to immediately inspect the new file proved greater than the need for lunch. Bryce flipped open the manila cover and started to read.

He had noted in Green's file that the dead man provided the police with incriminating evidence against Leonard Attwater. Now, in this second file, Bryce saw that although Attwater had been convicted of the same charge as Green, he had received a sentence of four and a half years – half as much again as Green's three years.

He sat back in his chair and summarised the likely scenario: a crook had been caught and had ratted on another crook in exchange for a reduced sentence. It was certainly a reasonable assumption that Attwater – the one ratted on – would bear a grudge against Green – the ratter.

More than that, reading Attwater's file Bryce saw that he had only been released two days earlier. The possibility that James Green's former partner had been festering away behind bars for an additional eighteen months, and planning retribution as soon as he was released, was not only plausible, he thought, but also somewhat likely. The urge to exact revenge, easily nurtured in the claustrophobic confines of prison walls, might dissipate quite quickly once a felon was released and enjoying his freedom again.

From what he knew so far, it seemed to Bryce that Attwater had struck without allowing the joys of release to blunt his desire for vengeance.

Happy to leave his desk and finally head towards the staff canteen, Bryce slipped back into his jacket and swung open his office door, almost walking into Constable Kittow, who had come to deliver the gun as instructed.

Again postponing lunch, Bryce had the gun lowered onto his office table, and scrutinised the automatic closely without touching it,

"This is an interesting piece – a Colt M1911, but chambered for the point four five five Webley cartridge. Remarkably, this one still has its serial number intact. If you don't know already, Kittow, the public could buy these, and the Government also bought them from Colt in the Great War, and I think for a long time afterwards. This one's stamped 'RAF', so it was bought after the Royal Flying Corps and Royal Naval Air Service merged to form the Royal Air Force. So we know we have a government purchased weapon, and an idea of when it was issued. We should be able to tell more of its history from the serial number.

"Make yourself useful again, Kittow, and see what you can find out about it. First, try for prints on the gun – especially the magazine – and the bullets in the magazine. The bullet from the baths is a non-starter, having passed through brain matter and two lots of bone. Possible chance on the magazine, very little chance on the pistol, and even less on the bullets, but you never know when you'll find a criminal who hasn't heard of fingerprints. A vanishing breed, sadly.

"Then, go and see the Armourer downstairs. Show him the gun and the bullet. Explain that this is a murder case and that you're working for me. He should be able to identify the armoury where the gun was proofed. I know the Royal Small Arms Factory in Enfield did them, but there may be others. There are stamps on here which I think identify that, but I'm not familiar with them. He can probably also tell you where the records – if any – are kept. They would show who, or at least which, unit was issued with this pistol after it was cleared by an inspector."

Kittow acknowledged his orders and set off.

Bryce realised he was now ravenous and had to go in search of sustenance when Sergeant Haig knocked on his door.

"Excellent timing, Haig, unless you've already had some lunch – in which case you can come and watch me eat; and give me your progress report at the same time."

Sergeant Haig hadn't in fact eaten. The two

men made their way to the canteen, collected a steaming plate of Irish stew each, and settled themselves in the now almost empty room. They had taken the last two portions of the day's main offering, but rather than finding it dried out, were pleasantly surprised that the lamb, vegetables and barley, had melded into an even more flavoursome meal than usual. Following Bryce's rule that whilst eating conversation should be general rather than shop, the detectives discussed the merits of the test series against New Zealand.

"Three days simply isn't long enough for a test match," opined Haig. Pity the New Zealanders refused the offer to play a fourth day in the last two tests, although I can understand their reasons. Could have had two results though, instead of four consecutive drawn matches."

"Agreed," replied Bryce. "But the 'timeless tests' before the war weren't invariably successful. I remember the one in Durban, when England needed nearly eight hundred to win, and reached six hundred and fifty-four for five, when they had to dash off to catch the ship home. That's still the highest fourth innings score in a first-class match."

The two discussed the brilliant performances of some of the players in the series – two lots of six wickets in an innings for Bailey, and the double hundred by Hutton at the Oval.

When they had only their mugs of tea to finish, the DCI returned to business.

"What did you find out at the baths, then?" he asked.

"A witness in the café – Katharine Hooper – knew Green by sight, and without any prompting said his name was Jimmy. According to Mrs Hooper, he was definitely in the café just before they closed up in there at ten last night. She recalled a man standing beside Jimmy's table, talking to him. But she only glimpsed him because she was pulling down the shutters on the counter at the time. She didnae see either of them again when she left, and she couldn't describe the other man, except he was wearing a dark coat, possibly a mackintosh. She remembered that particularly because it was a very warm evening and people just weren't wearing coats yesterday."

"Hmm. Good deep pockets in a coat, if you're carrying a gun." said Bryce.

"She told me that because the rest of the building is so secure the kitchen itself is never locked, only the provisions rooms. I suppose that might be relevant."

"Agreed," said Bryce, stirring his tea to cool it. "If these two were last in the café, it'd be pretty safe for our gunman to force Green into the kitchen, and then wait until everyone else had gone."

"But if the kitchen is where Green was cornered, sir, why not just shoot him in there and leave it at that?" queried Haig.

"A couple of possible reasons, I think. One is

that Green may have managed to make a bit of a run for it, and reached where he was found in the pool before he was shot.

"Alternatively, Attwater may have marched him around the pool at gunpoint so that he could be closer to the exit and make his getaway more quickly. Attwater knew his gun would make a noise and perhaps attract attention – he would have wanted to be as quick and sure of his escape as he possibly could be."

Haig nodded.

"Did you have any luck at Ranston Street?"

"Nothing inside that I could see would help us; no papers or anything else, unfortunately. Green rents his basement flat, and I'll tell you, sir, it's a proper wee pigsty inside – the sort of place where you use the doormat to wipe your feet on the way out, rather than the way in.

"According to an old neighbour who was more than willing to talk, Green's been living there since well before the war. This Mrs Roper told me there was a wife once, but she left when he went to prison and hasn't been seen again. The neighbour knew all about him. She said the LMS Railway sacked him when he was convicted, and he hasn't had a job since.

"But here's the thing, sir, she also said..." Haig shifted his position now. Leaning forward theatrically he assumed a knowing leer, tapped the side of his nose with a forefinger and transformed his mild Scots lilt for a London accent and said "'somehow, he's always paid his rent reg'lar. Howd'ya fink he done that then?'"

Bryce smiled at the caricature and nodded seriously.

"Yes, that certainly is interesting. We need to find out how Green managed to pay his rent all through his jail term when his wife had gone. Also, how he's managed to do it since he was released, if he hasn't worked.

"I have two bits of news myself, Haig. First, Kittow found the pistol. It's a British issue Colt four fifty-five automatic. Possibly won't help us, but he's trying to track its history.

"Second, Green was a 'grass'. As a direct result of information laid to our colleagues back in 1944, a man named Leonard Attwater was convicted and got a lengthy sentence – he came out a couple of days ago."

"That is good news, sir. I have to say I didnae hold out any hope at all for the bin search." Haig drank some tea, "And it's looking pretty bad for this Attwater bloke, isn't it?"

"Certainly isn't looking good for him, Sergeant. Which DC do you have with you?"

"Yapp, sir" replied Haig.

"Okay. I want the two of you to bring Attwater in. He's got rid of this gun, and there's nothing in his previous record to suggest he might have a stock of them. But you can go and collect a pistol if you'd like."

"No, sir, I'd prefer not. What's the address?"

Bryce dictated the address from memory and Haig made a note in his pocketbook.

"Even if he still lives in Petworth Street, chances are he won't be in, of course. See what you can glean from neighbours and so on. That'll warn him of our interest, unfortunately, if someone tips him off that we're sniffing around, but it's an eggs and omelette situation. If he is alerted by a well-wisher and then scarpers, we'll just have to put out an all-stations call to round him up.

"If you do find him, Haig, invite him to go with you to Battersea police station – it's only a few yards. If he refuses, you can arrest him on suspicion of the murder of James Green and get him to the station that way. Give me a call if you get him, and I'll come down. I'll contact 'V' Division to tell them what you're doing in their patch."

Haig confirmed he understood, drained his mug, and set off to round up Constable Yapp.

****

Back in his office, Bryce spent the next hour dealing with yet more paperwork which had arrived whilst he was at lunch. A call from Dr Bates at St Mary's Hospital interrupted him.

"Absolutely nothing special to report from the PM, Philip, everything was as we discussed earlier. Cause of death was the bullet, no question," said the police surgeon. "There was no water in the lungs, so he certainly died before falling or being pushed into the pool."

"As I said, the immersion means fixing the time of death is tricky, but I'm sticking to my original estimate of between 10 pm and midnight."

"Your estimate is sound, Paul. We have reason to believe the shot was heard at 10:45."

"Good. Always pleased to know I've earned my corn for the day and, as a taxpayer myself, that the Government isn't wasting its revenue money on me! Did you find the bullet?

"Yes, and the weapon – a point four five five Colt."

"Better and better, Philip. That ties in exactly with the entry and exit wounds," said the doctor. "You shall have my written report first thing tomorrow. Toodle-pip until we meet again, old boy!"

Bryce smiled as he hung up. There was something very engaging about the police surgeon. He was sure Veronica would warm to him as well, and made a mental note to ask if she would organise dinner invitations for Paul and his wife.

Bending over his paperwork, he was beginning to make headway with it again, when there was a knock at the door, and Kittow returned, his notebook filled with points to be relayed to the DCI.

"There were no prints at all on either gun or magazine, or bullets; all wiped clean. No chance on the fatal bullet, sir," he began.

"Inspector Bailey in the Armoury confirms what you said about the pistol." Kittow consulted his notes, "It's a Colt M1911, delivered to the RAF at some time after 1918, but possibly as late as 1942. The stamp was Enfield, as you thought, sir. In fact, the Armourer says he can even identify the inspector's initials, and from those he may be able to narrow the date down a bit more. He's making enquiries of Enfield now, sir. Then he's agreed to contact the War Department and the RAF himself – says he has the contacts and he'll be quicker than I could do it.

"He also suggests letting the Hendon lab fire a shot or two into their tank, and compare those bullets with the one you found.

"Depending on how much proof you need, he says there are still six rounds in the magazine. He suggests the lab could analyse the bullet you found and compare it to one in the magazine. Not definite proof, but apparently the chemical composition of bullets can vary significantly between batches, and it might be useful to prove these are identical."

"Thank you, Kittow," said Bryce, delighted with both the detail of the information and also the Constable's delivery of it. "Excellent, in fact. We'll almost certainly use Hendon, but I guess the Armourer wants to keep the pistol for a bit while he makes enquiries. I don't have any other tasks for you at present, so you go back to whatever you were doing before Sergeant Haig roped you in to help us out."

After a further half hour of pushing papers, the Chief Superintendent rang and asked for an update on the case. Bryce provided the salient points and added "I hope to make an arrest later today, sir."

He had hardly replaced the receiver when the telephone rang once more.

"Haig here, sir. Just to report we've got Attwater at Battersea. No trouble bringing him in – just told him you'd appreciate a chat. We haven't mention Green or said anything about murder. Attwater said he'd heard of you, and to use his exact words: 'I'd like to meet him, your Mr Bryce'."

"On my way," replied the DCI, wondering if his suspect would feel the same way when he was charged with murder.

****

As Haig had taken their usual Wolseley, Bryce picked up the keys for a pool car. Arriving at Battersea police station, he found Haig and Yapp talking to the Custody Sergeant.

"We've left him in an interview room, sir," said Haig. "He seems remarkably calm for a man about to be charged with a capital offence."

"Well, let's go and see him," replied Bryce. "You can come too, Yapp, good experience for you."

The three officers entered the interview room. Leonard Attwater was pacing around the small room in a leisurely manner as they came in.

He was a small and wizened man, dressed neatly but in cheap clothing. From his records Bryce knew Attwater was 48, but he could have passed for 60 easily.

To DC Yapp's surprise Bryce extended his hand to Attwater.

"Take a seat, Mr Attwater,"

The 'Mister' was equally surprising, and this time Yapp shot a questioning glance at Sergeant Haig, who smiled back at him and inclined his head slightly to signal 'watch and learn'. Haig knew that the DCI felt suspects often let their guards slip when they were treated with courtesy and less like suspects. Haig also knew that his boss would drop the velvet glove treatment and go in very hard, if he felt that would be more productive.

"Heard about you, guv. You've had dealin's with one or two of my mates," said Attwater, sitting down opposite Bryce and crossing his legs. "Very pleased to meet you at last."

If Attwater wanted to engage Bryce in conversation about his 'one or two mates' the DCI was having none of it. Ignoring the comment, he came straight to the point:

"We want a bit of help from you. Tell us about Jimmy Green."

"What's to tell?" asked Attwater, apparently supremely indifferent to Jimmy Green's name, and displaying nothing whatsoever in his manner or voice to show that he was in any way uncomfortable with the subject that Bryce wanted to discuss.

"He's a lousy grass, as you must know already," Attwater continued. "Split on me nearly five years ago, he did. No evidence until he grassed me up. A right little wrong-un, Green is. Haven't seen him since we went down at the Bailey together. We was in different nicks. I did my time in Wandsworth, but he lived north of the river, so I guess he went to Pentonville – but you'd know that better than me, wouldn't you? So, why d'you ask, Mr Bryce?"

"What do you know about automatic pistols?" was the DCI's response, as he ignored Attwater's question and put his own.

"Sweet. Fanny. Adams." came the deliberate reply. "I just missed the first war an' was too unfit this last time, so I never had to take up arms for the King – an' I'm glad. I've never touched weaponry of any sort. Not my style. Why you askin' me all this?"

"Simple. Green was shot dead late last night. In the back of the head. Executed, really, you might say." Bryce leaned forwards, his steady grey eyes holding the old lag's bloodshot brown ones, "I'm looking for his executioner, Mr Attwater."

Attwater remained impassive, and then slowly smiled.

"Oh, I see. There's you thinking just 'cos I'm fresh out of clink – after a long stretch inside that Green helped arrange – I must have done 'im in. Well, you can leave it out, Mr Bryce," said Attwater flatly.

"The most I'll admit to is hating the little bleeder; and there's no law says I can't do that. But risk the eight o'clock walk for him? He wasn't worth it!"

There was a measure of contempt in Attwater's voice that was extremely convincing.

"An' another thing. 'Til you told me, I didn't even know the little dirt-bag was dead. But now I do, I'm not gonna say a rosary for his soul tonight."

Attwater now made a performance of leaning towards Bryce and holding his gaze, clearly mimicking the DCI's earlier action.

"An' you'll 'ave to keep looking for his executioner, won'tcha, Mr Bryce?"

A deep silence fell over the little room. Bryce's every instinct was telling him that he had the wrong man in front of him; and that Attwater was enjoying the fact that his Sergeant and Constable had just witnessed a failed interrogation. Before he could turn his questioning around to alibis, Attwater took the initiative:

"But you said 'late last night'. What sort of time do you mean? An' where? 'Cos, as it happens, I've got a watertight alibi for most of yesterday." Attwater threw his head back and gave a belly-laugh, "So watertight it's bloomin' ocean-goin'!"

"I see," said Bryce. "It was in Marylebone. You'll need cover from about 10 o'clock to after midnight. And not anything supplied by your nearest and dearest," he added, with the justifiable cynicism of most policemen when told of a 'watertight' alibi."

"Oh, that's okay then," said Attwater, making no attempt to conceal his enjoyment of confounding the DCI's expectations.

"From about eight o'clock last evening until nine o'clock this morning I was in St Thomas's Hospital. Taken in with really bad belly ache. Doubled over. First they thought it was me appendix; they was talkin' about takin' the knife to me. Then a more senior geezer took a butcher's, and he didn't agree. Asked me a load of questions. In the end he was laughin'. Said I'd eaten and drunk too much all at once after bein' on prison grub for so long, and me belly couldn't cope. They didn't do the op – just give me somethin' to loosen me up. An' it didn't half work. By this mornin' the pain had gone, and they kicked me out.

"You can find a dozen doctors an' nurses at Tommy's, who can say that I was there – either in a bed or in the khazi – for all the time you're looking at. An' if ten o'clock is crucial, well that's about the time the senior doctor saw me. Sorry, to disappoint you, guv!"

Bryce was indeed disappointed, but philosophical. His investigation had taken a wrong turn and he would have to go back over everything and see where he made that wrong turn.

"Fair enough, Mr Attwater," he said, pleasantly. "But you must admit you look like the perfect suspect. We'll check your alibi, of course, but you're free to go now."

"Okey-doke, Mr Bryce. I'll not wish you luck in finding whoever shot Jimmy though." Attwater stood up and tucked his chair neatly under the table.

"Sayin' this in the nicest possible way, Mr Bryce, now I've met you, I 'opes never to see you again!"

Shaking hands with the DCI once more, and nodding cheerfully to the other two detectives, Attwater strode cockily out of the room. Bryce could imagine the conversation in the pub later that night, as Attwater regaled his 'one or two mates' with details of his interrogation.

"Do you believe him, sir?" asked DC Yapp.

"Oh yes," replied Bryce. "Very annoying, but there it is. My fault entirely. I saw what I believed was the link: the grudge, and the fact that he'd only just got out after serving time thanks to Green – and jumped to a conclusion that was plainly wrong.

"Even so, we need to check that alibi thoroughly. Sergeant, take Yapp, and call round to Tommy's now. Take this photo of Attwater I've got from Records. Bit out of date, but it's still a good enough likeness for anyone who saw him very recently. Make sure that he was there at the salient time; and that it wasn't someone else pretending to be him. Ideally, see if they can find you something – a document or anything that he touched. If there is, bring it back to the Yard and we can check the prints.

"My gut feeling tells me to believe his story, even though I don't want to. But I need to be absolutely certain all the same that I haven't just been fed a fairy tale."

"When you're satisfied at the hospital, both of you can go home. Assuming his alibi holds up, it's start again from square one for us tomorrow, I'm afraid."

****

Back at his desk, Bryce found a message asking him to call the Armourer. Feeling he had had enough time on the telephone for one day, he decided to visit Freddie Bailey in person and made his way to the Armoury. Handshakes and greetings exchanged, Bryce asked:

"What can you tell me?"

"Quite a bit, actually, Philip. First, the pistol was originally issued to an RAF Wing Commander in 1921. He was serving in the Middle East and so on. As you probably know, it was quite common for fliers to carry sidearms, in case they were shot down.

"Anyway, it seems he held on to it when he left the service, and gave it to his son, also an RAF pilot, sometime in the last war. The son, now Squadron Leader Metcalfe, was flying missions over enemy territory in Mosquitos."

"The son didn't draw a fresh pistol then?" queried Bryce.

"Apparently not. He preferred to trust his father's M1911, which had hardly ever been used, but was properly maintained. In fact the barrel is still pristine now, nearly thirty years after it was made.

"Actually, it was quite possible that he'd have been given an identical gun anyway, if he'd asked for one, as the model was still very much in service. In the father's day, officers could easily keep sidearms when they left the service. Nothing unusual there. And when the younger Metcalfe left the RAF in 1946, he didn't officially have a gun anyway. He just took it back home, and put it in a drawer."

The DCI nodded. The details he was hearing of how the Metcalfes shared the one gun all made sense, even if the arrangement was a little unorthodox.

"This is where we come to the interesting bit for you. Four days ago, someone broke into his house, in Lee Park, Blackheath. The pistol, kept in a desk drawer with a box of ammo, was taken, although very little else was. The burglary was reported to the local police.

"Your business entirely, Philip, but I'd put money on the gun either being stolen to order, or taken by the killer in person.

"Anyway, do you want me to get it to Hendon, so they can run some tests?"

"Yes please, Freddie. I thought we had our man already, but he seems to have an unshakeable alibi. In any case, he was in prison until three days ago, so it certainly wasn't him doing the burglary in person."

Somewhat buoyed by the latest news, Bryce decided it was time to go home.

****

The next morning the DCI arrived in the office at eight fifteen. Sergeant Haig was only a few minutes behind.

"Sit down, Sergeant, and tell me if Attwater's alibi holds up."

"It does, sir, every last detail of it. There's no doubt that he was in St Thomas's for the whole of the time he said. And one of the registrars, Mr Appleby, saw him at a quarter to ten. It was Appleby who correctly diagnosed the trouble, vetoed the operation, and prescribed Attwater a massive laxative, sir.

"Time he'd taken the dose it was gone ten. Even if he'd run straight out of hospital – and in his condition I don't think he'd dare – and even assuming he was already carrying the gun, he couldn't have been in the baths by last admissions."

"Fair enough. Well, I have a bit more news. The pistol was taken in a burglary four days ago. It looks as though it was the burglary target, as practically nothing else was stolen. And obviously Attwater couldn't have taken it as he was still in Wandsworth at the time.

"There are, of course, no prints on gun, magazine, or bullets. So, here are the tasks for today, Sergeant,"

Haig took out his pocketbook and pencil and readied himself.

"One. Take the prints you found on the pool door down to the fingerprint boys, and let them see if they can recognise anybody at all from them. With Attwater looking such a hot prospect yesterday, there wasn't any point in trying to match any prints from the door. It's a very long shot that you'll find any match at all, but give it a try.

"Two. Young Kittow seems quite competent. Send him to the baths, and tell him to take formal statements from the Superintendent, the café witness, and both ticket clerks.

"In particular, Carlo's statement needs to include the time he heard the 'noise'. He didn't say his wife heard it, but if she did, she can make a short statement too.

"The café witness needs to expand as much as she can about 'Jimmy' and the man she saw with him. Whether he was wearing gloves, for example. If he wasn't, he might have put his hands on the table. One hopes the table will have been wiped several times since then, for hygiene reasons. Just helpful from our point of view if it hasn't.

"Three. Since Green came out, he hasn't been in trouble – as far as we know. So, when you've sent Kittow on his way, I want you to go to Marylebone police station. Talk to the custody sergeant, and see if he knows anything about Green's doings. Get him to ask around too. Find out who the beat officer is for the Ranston Street area. If he's available, talk to him. If not, leave a message for him to contact one of us as soon as possible. Then go back to Ranston Street yourself. See your Mrs Roper again, and see if she can tell us anything about Green's friends. And try and find a few other talkative neighbours.

"I want to know what Green has been doing all day and all night since his release, who he associated with, and where he got the money to pay his rent.

"Four. I'm going to try to get hold of the Divisional Detective Inspector for 'R' Division. He may not even be aware yet of the connection between his case and ours. If I can see him at his office, and actually look at the file, so much the better.

"I want to find out more about this burglary. The thief knew the pistol was there. Someone in the house either spoke out of turn, or actually faked the burglary. It'll be interesting to see if there are servants in the house. I'm sure the DDI won't mind my interviewing anyone living there.

"I know I was wrong yesterday about Attwater, but I'm quite certain that the gun was taken specifically to carry out this murder. And it would seem that whoever did it was sufficiently familiar with Green's movements to know that he would be in the baths that evening.

"Five. After my false assumption about Attwater, I don't want to make another. I'm getting the lab boys to fire some shots from the pistol into their water tank, and prove definitely that the bullet you found did come from the gun. Inspector Bailey has that job in hand.

"Now, any comments?"

"Mrs Roper said Green's wife disappeared after he was sent down, but I don't suppose they've spent money on getting a divorce. If Mrs R has an address for Mrs G, it might be worth finding her. I suppose she should be told about the murder anyway."

"Good point, Sergeant. See what you can find out."

"Just one more thing, sir," said Haig. "Bertha Morland at the Bryanston entrance said he bought a washing ticket fairly regularly. If the killer knew he would be there at ten o'clock on a Monday night, we could ask questions next Monday night at the same time – chances are some other regular might know him."

"Yes, that's another good point, but I'll be very disappointed and think that we're losing our edge if we haven't got this one solved by next Monday!" said Bryce.

"In any case, we really do need to talk to people who were in the baths, or more particularly the café, yesterday evening, rather than other Mondays.

"We'll see what each of us finds during the day, and then decide if it may be worthwhile having a couple of people asking around in the baths this evening."

Haig left to carry out his instructions. Bryce picked up the telephone and asked the Yard switchboard operator to get the Greenwich police station. The operator made the connection for him via the exchange.

"Good morning," he said when the telephone was answered. "Detective Chief Inspector Bryce here; is your DDI in the office by any chance?"

It seemed that he was, and a few seconds later the DDI, an old acquaintance, was on the line.

"'Morning Adam, Philip Bryce here. Can I talk to you about a burglary in Lee Park?"

"Hello Philip; long time no speak – and even longer time no see! Yes, a Colt automatic was taken. I heard only a few minutes ago that a similar one was used to kill someone a couple of days later, so I was going to contact you shortly anyway. Is it the same gun?"

"Seems so, yes. It was found in a dustbin a few yards from the killing. Calibre matches. Hendon will do some test shots, but it's pretty certain."

"When my DS realised only the gun and a clock had been taken," said the DDI, "he assumed one of the two was stolen to order, and reported back to me. Since the gun was kept out of sight and the ornamental clock wasn't, we didn't struggle to decide it was the gun that was the intended haul, and the clock an opportunistic lift. But we haven't got anywhere as yet with finding the thief. No excuses, except we're very busy right now and undermanned, of course."

"Are you happy that I come and talk to your DS, Adam, and perhaps interview the Metcalfe chap? Servants too, if there are any?"

"Absolutely. Glad of your help, Philip. DS Gribble is here now; if you're coming immediately, I'll tell him to sit tight and wait for you. I'll probably see you myself, too, unless something else comes up."

****

Bryce drove over Westminster Bridge and joined the Dover Road, which took him all the way to Greenwich.

The desk sergeant recognised him, and confirmed DDI Egerton was expecting him. He instructed a nearby constable to show Bryce the way. They went upstairs and along a corridor, the constable tapping on the last door. There was a shout of "come in."

Egerton greeted his colleague with a smile and a hearty handshake. To the constable, he gave instructions.

"Find us three coffees please, Littlechild, and put your head into the CID office and ask Sergeant Gribble to join us here.

"Take a seat, Philip. How are things at HQ?"

"Always hectic, Adam. I do envy you here sometimes. Nicer office than mine, and almost the ruler of your Division. But I suppose you have your superintendent always breathing down your neck."

"That's so, although I'm lucky in that my boss leaves me alone to get on with the job."

"But tell me, is it true that the Met's most eligible bachelor has been snapped up and no longer available? Broken hearts all round the Yard's typing pool, I don't doubt!"

"Bryce grinned. "I might have known the grapevine would be working. Yes, the wedding was a fortnight ago; this is my first week back from honeymoon.

Seeking to turn the conversation away from himself, he said "I hear your status is also changing soon, Adam. They tell me that DDIs are to be abolished."

"Quite right, Philip; I'm to become a Detective Chief Inspector like you."

A knock at the door heralded a middle-aged man wearing a light grey suit. Stepping into the room, he held the door open for Constable Littlechild, who followed bearing a tray with three mugs of coffee.

"This is First Class Detective Sergeant Gribble, said Egerton. "Gribble, meet DCI Bryce."

The two officers shook hands.

"Well, Sergeant, you've heard that the pistol

taken from the Lee Park burglary was used to kill a man in Marylebone yesterday. While you want to solve a burglary case, my case looks like a gangland execution, and I want enough evidence to prosecute someone. What can you tell me?"

Gribble looked at his boss, but Egerton said "you start."

"It's a big house, sir, on four levels. Squadron Leader Metcalfe lives there with his parents. I was told that technically the gun belongs to the father, a retired Group Captain, but it was used by the son in the last war. Actually, being pedantic, it belongs to the RAF, sir, but never mind.

"Both Metcalfes share a big study on the ground floor, and each of them has a desk. The pistol was kept in the son's desk. Unlocked drawer, sir," said Gribble, shaking his head to indicate that he thought Metcalfe ought to have known better.

"He said the pistol wasn't loaded, but admits there was a box of ammunition kept with it.

"The study has glazed doors opening onto the back of the house. They were forced, undoubtedly from the outside, and probably by a professional burglar. It's not hard to get access to the garden.

"No fingerprints apart from those of the household. There was no disruption of any kind, and it was obvious that the burglar knew exactly where to go. Apart from the pistol, the only other item taken was a fancy mantel clock from the same room. Obviously, the prime purpose was to get the Colt.

"The household consists of the three Metcalfes, and two live-in staff, maids really, although one of them says she does some 'plain' cooking. There's also another woman who comes in three times a week to help with cleaning. We've spoken briefly to all three servants – all deny any knowledge.

"Now I'm not making excuses for the delay, sir, and we realised at once that the pistol was likely taken for a specific purpose. But the DDI will confirm that we do have several other urgent cases running, and nowhere near enough men. Anyway, I'm due to go back to the house later today to do proper interviews."

There was silence for a minute as Bryce absorbed this information and then gave his assessment:

"So, the assumption is that the pistol was stolen to order, by a professional burglar, and that old habits caused him to take the clock as well. That certainly seems likely."

This time Egerton replied. "That's right," he said. "Let's assume your killer needs a gun. He's heard where one can be found. If he is doing the burglary himself, no way would he take anything else, and especially not a highly distinctive clock – it would carry far too much risk when it was fenced, even months down the line. So we don't think he did the job himself.

"He asks around for, or more probably

already knows, a burglar. And I bet he said not to take anything other than the pistol. But his light-fingered pal sees something that takes his fancy."

"Can't disagree with that hypothesis, Adam," sad Bryce. "So, two things: first, can you pull in a few likely burglars for questioning, and second, can I go with Sergeant Gribble to see these people?"

"Yes to both," replied Egerton. "Another DS is organising the possible burglars as we speak. And even if we don't find our man amongst those that we bring in, I think we stand a better chance of someone either welching, or making a nomination, now there's a capital charge in the offing.

"I look forward to learning from you, sir," said Gribble with a smile.

"Actually, I was proposing to sit at the back of the room and let you conduct the interviews," said Bryce. "After all, the burglary is your case. But we can play it by ear."

****

While his boss was in the Greenwich police station, Sergeant Haig was sitting in the small front room of a house in Ranston Street, talking to the woman he had seen the previous day. Mrs Roper was again being friendly, but it became obvious that although her suspicions about Green were strong, they were not evidence.

"Is there anyone else who could help me

with some hard facts about Jimmy, Gladys? asked Haig.

"Well, there's Aggie Bishop," said the woman after a moment's thought. "She's split from her old man now, can't blame her – never liked 'im meself – but her Terry and Jimmy were close. Not friends exactly, but thick as thieves, as the sayin' goes. Far as I know, Jimmy just worked for Terry at something. Terry's a right crook o' course, so whatever it was Jimmy did for 'im it weren't an honest day's work.

"The Bishops moved away a couple o' years ago. Money, they 'ad. Went to live in a flat in Hamilton Terrace. Walked past to look once – reely posh it is. But when they split, Aggie comes back to this street, though not the same house they used to 'ave. I s'pose he makes her an allowance.

"They never 'ad kids," she added inconsequentially, before disclosing "and when I say Terry was Aggie's old man, I'm not sayin' they tied the knot and got a legal sustificate – 'opped over a broomstick, more like."

Mrs Roper fell silent for a while. She was old enough to be Haig's mother, and seemed to have taken a maternal shine to him. She made a decision to be more helpful:

"Look Sarge, you wait here, an' I'll go and see if she's in an' ready to talk. Won't take two shakes of a lamb's tail."

Gladys was true to her word, and reappeared very quickly. Following her into the little living room was a dowdy middle-aged woman with a suspicious expression on her face. Haig stood and introduced himself, and the three sat down.

"I've never been no copper's nark and I'm not about to start today," said Aggie forthrightly. "So, you tell me why you want to know about Jimmy, before I talk."

Haig looked at Gladys in surprise, "Haven't you told her about Jimmy?" he asked.

"Nope," replied the older woman, "left that for you."

"And you haven't read today's papers?" he asked Aggie.

"Never read 'em," answered the woman. "Truth is, I don't read good anyways."

Oh, right," said Haig. "Brace yourself then – Jimmy was shot dead the night before last."

"Blimey o' Reilly!" said Aggie, apparently genuinely astonished. "Well, well, well. Still, 'ad it coming to 'im, I guess."

"How's that, Aggie?" asked Haig, sensing that something worthwhile was about to be revealed.

Aggie looked at him for some time, apparently weighing up how much to say.

"He liked to put the squeeze on," she said eventually. "Terry said that Jimmy'd got to know how a rich geezer made money in the war, not legal like, and how he wouldn't want that known now he was trying to be respeckable.

"My Terry's not straight – every copper

in the district knows that – and Jimmy had something on him too, although I never found out what. Fact is that Terry warned him off a year or two ago for trying the black on 'im – I was there and heard it all. Told Jimmy he'd never pay a blackmailer, least of all 'im, and that if he ever opened his trap he'd shut it forever. Terry never bore a grudge, though. Still gave Jimmy little jobs to do from time to time. Keepin' an eye on 'im. I shouldn't wonder.

"But don't run away with the idea that Terry killed him, Sarge. No way. He might have threatened, but he's never been violent, not even to me in the middle of some right barneys."

Haig extracted Terry's address from Aggie with some difficulty, on the understanding that the police wouldn't mention her involvement. Privately, he thought that Terry Bishop would put two and two together without much trouble, but he refrained from saying so.

Thanking the women, the Sergeant left to return to the Yard.

****

Gribble and Bryce travelled to Blackheath in separate cars, Gribble leading, although the DCI had already checked a map to see where Lee Park was. As he drove, Bryce pondered the status of a 'First Class Sergeant'. One in uniform wore a crown above his three stripes, exactly like a staff sergeant in the army. But a CID man had nothing to show for his rank except a few extra shillings each week and a clumsy title which people never used when addressing him.

They drove a little further out along the Dover Road before turning off across the heath into Blackheath village. Passing the railway station, Gribble drove up the hill and forked right at the top, into a tree-lined road with very large houses on both sides. He turned into the driveway of a typical example.

"Don't introduce me unless someone specifically asks," Bryce instructed the Sergeant, when they got out of their cars in front of the house. "Let each person know the gun has been used in a murder. And if either of us gets the feeling that someone is hiding something, then we go in hard. If necessary, we take that person to the station. Okay?"

"Fine by me, sir," replied Gribble, using a large ornate knocker to let the occupants of the house know they had visitors.

A woman of about forty, dressed in a black uniform with a white apron and a cap, opened the door.

"Hello, Sergeant, thought we'd see you again," she greeted them. "Come in. Who did you want to see?"

"Everyone who might be in at the moment," replied Gribble. "You first, if you can spare us ten minutes."

"The Group Captain is at home, but Mrs

Metcalfe and the Squadron Leader are both out. I'd better take you into the small parlour where you saw us before."

She led them a few yards along the hallway, and into a room which had the appearance of a dentist's waiting room, even to the extent of a pile of magazines laying on the mahogany table. They all sat down, the officers facing the woman.

"For the record, Violet, just tell us your full name and address," began Gribble."

"Violet Hanson, Sergeant, and this is my address."

Gribble asked a few questions about the house, its residents, and its routines. Then he suddenly said:

"The stolen gun was used to murder someone a couple of days ago. That makes this a very, very serious matter, Violet."

"That's awful," replied the maid, "I hope it was a bad person who got killed. But I don't know anything about it. I didn't even know there was a gun in the house. When you came before you said it was in the study. Well, I don't ever clean the study, and the only time I ever go in there is to take tea or coffee or something to the Master or the Squadron Leader. Never seen a gun, nor heard talk of one."

Bryce, sitting behind the maid, shook his head when Gribble glanced at him.

"All right, Violet, ask Hannah to come along, please. Also, out of courtesy, please tell the Group

Captain that we are here – but don't mention the murder to either of them just yet."

Several minutes passed before a girl knocked at the door and, reluctantly, came into the room. She looked to be about sixteen, and was dressed in a similar way to Violet.

Sergeant Gribble invited her to sit, and asked for her details.

"Hannah Lane, sir, and I live here," she replied, apparently close to tears.

Gribble looked at her without speaking for a full minute, and she visibly began to squirm.

"You knew about the gun, didn't you Hannah?" He shot the question at the girl. She had barely had time to nod when he fired the next:

"When did you first see it?"

Hannah was now crying openly. "Months ago, sir," she stammered, swallowing hard as her tears flowed down her cheeks.

"How? Was it on the desk?"

"No, I had to clear some paper fasteners off the desk one day before I could dust. I opened the drawer and sort of swept them in. That's when I saw the gun."

"I see," said Gribble. "Did you pick the gun up?"

"No! Oh no! I wouldn't dare touch a gun," cried the girl.

"Things are worse now than when I was here before, Hannah," Gribble went on, "the gun was used to murder someone. That makes this a hanging matter."

It seemed hardly possible, but Hannah's crying became even more intense.

"Now, we know that someone in this house told somebody outside the house about this gun, and exactly where it was kept.

"That was you, Hannah, and you're upset because you know you helped in the burglary, whether you meant to or not," continued Gribble.

The girl nodded through her tears. "I didn't mean to," she wailed.

Bryce now spoke from behind her, making her jump. She turned in her seat to face him.

"Hannah, we can take you to the police station right now and charge you with being an accessory before the fact – that means that you were involved in doing something to assist in this burglary and probably the murder. If we do that you'll be locked up and brought before a court.

"But if you tell us who you talked to – and when – I think we can keep you out of this."

Hannah, who hadn't stopped sobbing, now let out another wail.

"I never meant no harm, sir," she cried. "Please don't put me in prison. A few days ago, on my evening off, I just mentioned it to a boy I know. In a pub in Deptford, we was."

"Who is he, Hannah," growled Gribble. "Come on now, time for the truth."

"Tony Finch," she stammered at last.

"Is he your boyfriend, Hannah? asked Bryce.

"Oh no, sir," she replied, I haven't got one. His girlfriend is someone I knew from school, that's how I know him."

"Who else heard you, Hannah?" asked Gribble.

"Nobody else; nobody at all was anywhere near us," the girl told them. "Tony's friend had gone to the bar to get drinks, and my friend had gone to the ladies. There was just him and me left at the table. I s'pose I told him about the gun to show off, like."

"Well," said Bryce, "we'll need you to come down to the station now, and sign a statement, but I promise that you won't be locked up and you'll be able to come back here within an hour."

"I won't see you at the station, Hannah – the Sergeant here will deal with you. But I'll just say one more thing. You aren't old enough to go into public houses!"

"No sir, thank you very much, sir," sniffled the dejected girl, looking just a little happier now the threat of imprisonment had lifted.

Gribble quickly wrote a few words on a clean sheet in his notebook, tore the sheet out and passed it to Bryce. After a quick scan the DCI smiled his appreciation at the Sergeant.

All three were now standing and ready to make a move, when a brief tap on the door was followed by a trim-looking man in his late sixties entering the room. Clean-shaven, grey haired, dressed in slacks and open-necked shirt with cravat, he looked searchingly from face to face.

"Good morning, Sergeant," he said. "Hope I'm not interrupting. Any progress?"

Bryce took charge.

"I think I'd better explain a few things to you," he said. "Let me just set something else in train first.

"Sergeant, I suggest you take Hannah and get her statement. Get someone to give her a lift back here afterwards. I'll call you later."

Gribble and the maid left the room.

"Perhaps we should sit down," said Metcalfe. "Now, I gather you are senior to Sergeant Gribble? I'm Group Captain Metcalfe, by the way."

"I'm Detective Chief Inspector Bryce, from Scotland Yard," said Bryce. "Your burglary is of interest to me only because of what was taken. The gun which was stolen from here was the weapon used two days ago to murder someone."

"Good God!" exclaimed Metcalfe. He thought for a moment. "What a mess. My son and I are at fault here, of course, and I don't seek to avoid blame, or even to offer mitigation.

"What's the position with young Hannah? She looked upset."

"It seems she accidentally saw the pistol months ago. Very recently she casually mentioned it to someone outside the house. Unfortunately, that person seems to be closely related to what we might call a professional burglar, although I don't want that known until we can pull the man in for questioning.

"I've promised Hannah that we wouldn't prosecute her as an accessory to either murder or burglary, if she provided a name. It's up to you, of course, but I hope you won't dismiss her. She saw the pistol when she cleared some paper clips from the desktop into the drawer – a pure accident, she wasn't prying. She meant no harm, and months later was basically showing off to impress a young man. You can safely assume she won't be so careless about your business again."

"Well, you're very persuasive, Chief Inspector. Certainly we have been quite satisfied with Hannah. I'll have to discuss it with my wife, though."

"Good. I'm sure your discussion will include the fact that had the gun been properly kept, Hannah would never have seen it," said Bryce very pleasantly, but also very pointedly.

Metcalfe sighed. "As soon as you told me your name, I remembered seeing your picture in the papers. Even in the second or so before you mentioned murder, I realised that you weren't here just about a burglary.

"So, will you be bringing any charges against Mark or me?"

"That's not in my hands, Group Captain," said Bryce. "The Divisional Detective Inspector will decide. But I think it's very unlikely. I don't think you'll be getting the pistol back, though!"

Bryce took his leave, and went back to his

car. Before starting the engine, he read Gribble's truncated note again, glad that the Sergeant hadn't spoken in front of Hannah.

'Tony Finch. Son of Spencer Finch. One of best burglars our patch. Only managed convict twice. Top of list to pull in.'

Bryce smiled, and started back towards Westminster. After pausing at a pub on the Dover Road for a ploughman's and a half pint of bitter for lunch, he returned to the Yard.

****

Haig arrived back at the Yard first, and left a note on the DCI's desk to say he was now in his own office. Twenty minutes later, Bryce called and asked him to come up.

"Anything useful? asked the DCI.

"Oh yes, I think so, sir," replied his Sergeant.

"Good, me too," said Bryce. "Let me start with the burglary that kicked things off, then you can tell me how it fits in with what you have."

He gave Haig a concise description of Hannah's admission, and the connection with the known burglar.

"The Greenwich boys will pull in this man Finch. I very much doubt if he is also the murderer, but they can use the fact that this is a capital case to persuade him to talk. What have you got?"

Haig reported Aggie Bishop's contribution.

"Shall we pull him in, sir?" he asked.

"Yes. And I think we'll have Terry Bishop

in here, and not at the local nick. He can start sweating a bit harder in the car on the way to the Yard; hopefully that will soften him up for the interview. When we've finished here, Haig, you take one of the DCs and find Bishop. Same procedure as Attwater: if he doesn't feel like co-operating, arrest him on suspicion of murder."

"Very good, sir," replied Haig. 'There's only a couple of other things, no use really. The Custody Sergeant at Marylebone knew Green by sight, and remembers him from when he was arrested back in 1944 – the Sergeant was only a constable back then. But he says there's nothing concrete come up on Green since. Later, I found the regular beat officer for the Ranston Street area. He described Green as having a shady reputation – rumours of wrong-doing circulating about him – but nobody has ever come up with anything to pin an offence on him since he came out.

"Right, you get off after Bishop. If you can't find him anywhere this afternoon, ask the Marylebone lads to keep an eye out and tell them to take him in on my authority whenever he turns up."

Haig left on his latest mission.

Bryce called the Greenwich station again and told DDI Egerton about the possible blackmail connection.

"I'm hoping to get the name of this 'respectable geezer' when we can find Bishop. No guarantee that this isn't another wild goose chase, of course, but it looks hopeful. Anyway, Adam, if you can persuade Finch that he'd better talk, it would be good to get Terry Bishop's name from him."

"Leave it with us, Philip. Gribble and I will interview Finch ourselves."

"Ah, the old good cop, bad cop, routine?"

"No, not for this charmer. Bad cop, bad cop, routine!" laughed Egerton.

"I was impressed with Gribble this morning, by the way," said Bryce. "He did very well with the Lee Park people."

"That's good to know, Philip. He was set to get the next DDI job. But now they're being abolished, he'll certainly be promoted to DI soon. Anyway, I'll keep you informed."

Telephone receiver replaced, Bryce turned his attention to his 'in' tray.

****

An hour later, the telephone rang.

"You owe me one, Philip," said the voice of Adam Egerton. "We got Finch in. As soon as we said we were looking for someone to hang, he was singing very sweetly. Named your man Bishop without prompting.

"Bishop had been putting the word around that he wanted a pistol outside of the usual channels. Finch mentions this to his son over the breakfast table in passing, as I suppose you might do when you're a family of crooks. The son, who's probably being brought up to take over from his dad, says words to the effect of 'that's a coincidence, last night I heard where you can pick one up'. The son is sent off to get the address via his girlfriend.

"Finch does a quick inspection of the house and gardens, sees it's an easy job for him, and breaks in the same night. Didn't intend to take anything else, but couldn't resist the clock – which he still has.

"Gets the word back to Bishop, who meets Finch in the Trafalgar Tavern in Greenwich. The gun is handed over, and Finch collects £175 in mostly new fivers and tenners. Chuffed and thinking it was the easiest money he'd ever made.

"He's admitted the burglary, so we're holding him on that. We could charge the son with being an accessory, but he's a juvenile and probably not worth it.

"And then, we have a last bit of luck. He had the money on him when we picked him up. I'll get one of my boys to phone through the serial numbers later – just a chance they can be traced.

"I think that makes this the first case in my career, Philip, where every single piece of evidence has fallen into my lap!"

"Pleased to hear that, Adam; your case completely cracked, and hopefully mine now cracking. Thanks again."

Bryce leaned back in his chair and smiled

to himself. After the first wrong assumption, this time it looked as though things were panning out well.

He didn't have long to wait for further movement. DC Yapp rang from the front desk:

"Yapp reporting sir. We have Terry Bishop for you. Found him at home."

"Well done, Yapp. I want him to sit and stew for a bit. Have you told him what this is about?"

"No sir, just that someone at the Yard wanted to talk to him. He kept asking questions on the way in, but Sergeant Haig wouldn't speak to him. Didn't need to arrest him, by the way, he came along quietly. He did ask at one point if he needed a mouthpiece, but Sarge carried on ignoring him."

"Excellent! Right Yapp, you go and sit in with him, and keep up the stony silent treatment. Ask Sergeant Haig to come up and see me."

Haig appeared a few minutes later, grinning widely.

"Horrible oily little man," he said. "If there weren't two of us, I bet he'd have tried a bribe. How are you going to play this, sir?"

"I want him to sweat for a bit. Then you and I will go in and talk to him about guns – see what he says on that subject. The Lee Park burglar has squealed, in fact, and named Bishop as buying the gun. Paid £175 in cash, and Greenwich are trying to trace the numbers as we speak. At the right moment, we'll lob that at him.

"The statement of Mrs Hooper at the café

says the man with Green was 'respectable' and 'smart'. Could Bishop be described in those terms?"

"Not at all, sir. Scruffy little beggar. Although he obviously makes a good bit of money – posh flat, gold tie pin, and so on – he still doesn't know how to dress."

Bryce rose and opened the door, "Miss Reynolds, be an angel and bring us a couple of teas, please."

"We'll have a break and then amble along to see our man," he said to Haig. The Sergeant nodded in appreciation – it was some time since anything had passed his lips.

****

Twenty minutes later, the two officers went down to the interview room where Yapp and Bishop were waiting, one noticeably nervous, and the other relaxed to the point of boredom. Bryce and Haig took seats opposite Bishop as Yapp moved to stand by the door.

The DCI stared at Bishop in silence for a full minute before suddenly asking:

"Do you know who I am?"

Bishop nodded hesitatingly.

"Then you know I wouldn't waste my time with you unless there was something important in it for me," said Bryce in a conversational tone. "Talk to me about pistols."

"Don't know what you mean, Mr Bryce," began Bishop. "I don't know nuffink about guns, no way. I 'ardly know one end of a gun from the other."

"Well, I have some doubts about that, Mr Bishop. But tell you what, we'll pretend I'm taking your word. For the moment." There was a steely edge to Bryce's voice which, together with his words conveyed a clear message to Bishop, who started to twitch about in his seat but said nothing.

"Let's not talk guns then – you being such a stranger to them. Let's talk about your old friend Jimmy Green instead."

"Nah, I wouldn't say 'friend', Mr Bryce. More like someone I see from time to time."

"Come off it, Terry. He put the 'black' on you, didn't he?"

Bishop was silent for a few seconds, obviously calculating what information the DCI might be holding.

"Jimmy did think 'e might have something that I'd pay him for," he said at last. "But if 'e'd tried to push it I'd have reported him to you to deal wiv, o' course. I wouldn't take the law into me own 'ands."

All three officers laughed derisively.

"He was bleeding you, Terry, and so you decided to finish him off."

"No, no, Mr Bryce, not me. I did see about it in the Standard this afternoon – shook me right up. But you can't pin that on me."

"Can't we? I think that's exactly what we'll

do, and in a couple of months we'll see you at the Bailey when the judge puts on his black cap."

Bishop's face paled even further, but he said nothing.

"I'll tell you what you did, shall I?" continued Bryce.

"You put the word out that you needed a pistol. And we certainly know what you wanted it for. You got the pistol, and you knew Jimmy well enough to predict where he's likely to be on a Monday evening. You meet him, and you shoot him in the back of the head. You dump the gun – which we found, by the way.

"Now, tell me where I've gone wrong."

"It's all wrong, guv, honest! I don't know about guns. I wouldn't know where to get hold of one. Yeah, I might not be completely straight – but I've never done no violence. Never. I don't hold with violence. I wouldn't know how to work one of them automatics anyway."

Bryce leaned forward, and smiled wickedly.

"How did you know it was an automatic pistol used to kill Jimmy?" he asked in a menacing tone.

Bishop began to shake. "Must've seen it in the papers," he stammered.

"No, you didn't, Terry. There's been no mention. So for all you knew it could have been a shotgun. Or a rifle. Or a revolver. Or even a Thompson machine gun. But somehow you knew it was an automatic pistol. Well, well, well. The noose is tightening, Terry."

"No, Mr Bryce, you got no proof! That was just me guessing about the gun."

"It wasn't a guess, Terry. You knew perfectly well it was an automatic, because you'd actually bought it, complete with ammunition, all ready to shoot poor Jimmy."

Bishop somehow tried to pull himself together. "No, sir," he said. "That you can't prove 'cos it didn't 'appen!"

"Wrong again," replied Bryce, giving Bishop what he hoped was a malevolent smile.

"You bought it from Saul Finch. You paid him £175. You collected it in the Trafalgar Tavern. We have the cash, and your dabs are all over it."

Bishop let out a groan, and put his head in his hands.

Sergeant Haig joined in:

"I think that'll be plenty for any jury, Terry. You were being blackmailed. You didnae like it. You put the word around that you needed a gun. You bought one. You shot the man who was blackmailing you." Turning to Bryce, Haig made another attempt to break Bishop, "We might as well book Mr Pierrepoint now, Chief Inspector."

Bishop jumped up from his chair. Bryce and Haig didn't move, but Yapp got ready to intervene. However, Bishop merely did a few circuits around the small room, and returned to his seat. He had made a decision.

He was about to speak, when the DCI

signalled to Haig to issue a formal caution. That done, Bryce's manner changed again and he said, quite gently:

"All right, Terry, you've got one chance only to tell us who wanted the gun."

Bishop's manner and voice were both completely panicked now:

"I hope you sort this right quick, gents, 'cos if he hears I'm in 'ere before you take him, I'm a dead man."

"Better trust us then, Terry, because if we don't get a name that we like better than yours, you're as good as dead anyway," said Haig.

There was a short pause.

"Danny Farrell," said Bishop at last, "bent as they come, but 'e's going up in the world now, pretends to be respectable like an'..."

Bryce held up a hand, "Hold up a moment." He turned to Yapp, "Nip along to Records and see what they have on this Danny Farrell.

"On you go, Terry. We're going to need a lot more yet." Bishop groaned, but continued:

"When Jimmy squealed on Lennie Attwater a few years ago, 'e could have given you Danny too, for the same job. An' Danny was higher in the ring. But 'e didn't, 'cos Danny could pay 'im to keep shtum.

"That's okay for a few years; Jimmy never 'ad much ambition like. But then 'e starts getting 'ooked on the dogs and nags, and 'is cost of livin' goes up. And I think maybe 'e finds out something more about Danny too – worth a lot more cash p'raps. Anyway, 'e tries to squeeze more 'n more from 'is meal ticket. Danny gets the 'ump.

"Calls me round to 'is 'ouse. Does all 'is business there. Tells me a bit about Jimmy. Tells me 'e's passing the word that 'e wants a gun with no history. Says for me to ask around quietly too. Then 'e says 'e doesn't trust no one else to do the akshul job, and 'e's got the guts to do it 'isself. Told me 'e needs to make an example of Jimmy. Took that to mean Jimmy wasn't the only one wiv 'is 'and in Danny's pocket.

"I'll go down for handling the gun, but I'll not swing. I didn't know this Saul Finch, but Danny must've 'eard somehow 'e could provide. Anyway, Danny told me where to go; he give me the cash and a pony for meself."

"You'll do eight or ten years for this, Terry – I shouldn't think a pony would make that worth your while," remarked the DCI.

"Too right, Mr Bryce, but it's a bit late to ask for a monkey now, innit?" Bishop added, with philosophical acceptance of his poor bargain.

"You're going straight to the cells from here, Terry. Later, we'll get a statement from you. After that, we'll start the charges against you, beginning with handling stolen property. Then we'll see how well your memory works before I decide whether to add accessory before the fact. Or conspiracy to commit murder." The DCI's voice was hard and uncompromising as he delivered his last thrust:

"And if this Farrell doesn't exist, or has a cast-iron alibi, we're looking to you for shooting Green."

"Oh, 'e exists orlright. An' my memory's coming back. When I took 'im the gun Danny's face lit up. He puts on some gloves, and then shakes out some ammo from the box to fill the magazine thing, put it back in then cocks it. 'E points the gun straight in my face an' says 'You know better than to talk, Terry, don'tcha?'."

Bishop passed a trembling hand over his lips at the memory and, for the first time, looked Bryce in the eye before adding in a piteous whisper:

"I nearly soiled meself, Mr Bryce, I was that scared cos 'e weren't joking. So you can lock me up. Good an' tight until you've got 'im behind bars."

****

Bryce had hardly sat down in his office when Yapp arrived carrying a file. "Farrell's record, sir," he reported.

"Thanks," said Bryce. Go down to the holding cells, and join Sergeant Haig taking Bishop's statement. When that's done, both of you come back here, and we'll see what needs doing next."

The DCI opened the file. It was thin, and although it showed four convictions, all were for comparatively minor offences. Three, all for theft of one sort or another, dated back to the years before the war. The most recent of these was in 1938, when Farrell had been given a sentence of four months. But in 1940 he had been given eighteen months for actual bodily harm and, reading between the lines, the sentence might well have been longer had the victim not been a man of extremely bad character himself.

Since then, there had been no further convictions, although there were notes regarding unproven allegations of intimidation, living off immoral earnings, and forgery – the last of course tying in with Bishop's claim that Farrell had been behind the uttering charges that Attwater and Green had done time for.

There were two mugshots, the most recent dating from the 1940 conviction. Assessing these, Bryce could see that Farrell was a handsome man – almost distinguished-looking.

There was an address in Marylebone given in 1940, but a handwritten note dated 1948 gave a different address – only a few hundred yards away from the first but, on checking a large-scale map, Bryce saw that this was a detached property, and substantially more upmarket. The map showed access to both front and rear.

He contemplated whether he and Haig needed to be armed. The British police never routinely carried firearms. On the other hand, if Bishop's story was true, the man they had to arrest had killed before. The fact that Farrell had wanted a 'new' gun for Jimmy didn't necessarily mean he didn't have another – or more. Bryce was also mindful of the old saying, 'you can only be hanged once'. If Farrell was successfully cornered, he might indiscriminately shoot his way out, thinking he had nothing to lose in doing so.

Eventually coming to a decision, the DCI went down to the armoury and sought out Inspector Bailey.

"Philip, I don't see you for months and now it's twice in two days! What are you after this time?"

"Same case, Freddie. But I want to arrest our suspected gunman, and I think we need to carry ourselves."

"Fair enough; I can do that on your written order. What do you fancy? I can do you a nice pump-action twelve bore, or even an ex-army Sten."

Bryce laughed. "Funnily enough, I mentioned a Tommy gun earlier today – you don't have one of those, I suppose?"

"I do, actually – choice of 20-round box magazine, or 50-round drum. Taken in a raid in the 1920s, and been here ever since. But even with the smaller mag it's too heavy for close up action, so I wouldn't recommend it."

"Very kind offers, Freddie, but I'll settle for a couple of automatic pistols. I have an M1911 at home – with a licence – can you match that?"

"Certainly can. Four fifty-fives, same as the one you sent down yesterday. Couple of boxes of ammo do you?"

"Yes, thanks."

"OK, just write me out a chit and I'll see what I can find."

Bailey returned a few minutes later. He took Bryce's chit, read it carefully, and then pushed two holstered automatics across the counter, together with two boxes of ammunition over-stamped with 'not for revolvers'.

"Good luck, Philip," he said. "I just wish my eyesight allowed me to work in the field."

"You won't say that if I'm shot, Freddie," replied Bryce, taking the guns and leaving the room.

Back in his office, he carefully checked both pistols, loaded them, and locked them away in a drawer.

Picking up the telephone, he asked to be put through to Marylebone police station. The DDI wasn't in, but when Bryce identified himself and asked for the loan of a couple of uniformed constables to assist with an arrest, the desk sergeant agreed without question. Bryce advised that either he or Sergeant Haig would pick the men up at the station in an hour.

Calling down to the transport down to the transport pool, he booked a second car.

When Haig and Yapp returned Bryce showed them the photograph of Farrell, and checked that the address in the records was the same as that given by Bishop.

He explained the arrangements he had in

mind.

"We'll take two cars. Rendezvous at Marylebone nick. We're collecting two local officers. You'll take one, Sergeant, and station yourselves at the back. I'll take Yapp and the other man and go in at the front.

"You and I will be armed, Sergeant." He took the pistols out of the drawer and pushed one across the desk to Haig. "It's already loaded. I know you've fired one of these in the range. If Farrell comes out of the back of the house with a gun in his hand it's because he's not responding to my invitation to give himself up at the front. So don't hesitate – shoot to kill, whether you've heard shots from the front or not. I don't want any bystanders hurt so no second chances for him. Questions?"

There were no questions. Bryce and Haig each put a pistol into a jacket pocket, and the spare ammunition into another, leaving the holsters on the desk.

****

The two cars pulled in at Marylebone police station. Bryce introduced himself to the two waiting constables, Dacre and Whymark. He explained what was to be done.

"If there's any shooting, don't try to be heroes," he said firmly. "Get behind the best cover you can as quick as you can. Sergeant Haig and I are carrying guns; leave it to us."

The journey took only four minutes. Bryce

parked fifty yards from Farrell's house. He gave Haig a few minutes to get in position, and then said "let's go."

The three men ran along and up the three steps to the front door. Bryce knocked loudly.

Footsteps could be heard approaching, and the door opened. The man inside saw the three on the step, and as one was a uniformed constable he realised they were police before Bryce could speak. Spinning round, he ran back along the hall.

"Get him," yelled Bryce, drawing his pistol. All three officers ran after the fleeing man. Farrell turned into a room off the hall and was diving into a desk drawer when Bryce, leading the charge, raised his pistol and shouted, "Stop, Danny, or I'll shoot!"

Farrell looked back, saw Bryce was indeed armed, and froze.

"Move over there against the wall," said Bryce, and without taking his eyes off Farrell, said "Yapp, keep well out of my line of fire, and take a look in those drawers."

Yapp quickly reported that he had found a pistol.

"Oh dear," said Bryce. "I'm glad you weren't carrying it when you answered the door, Danny. Anyway, you're under arrest on suspicion of murder.

"Whymark, without spoiling my nice direct line of fire, cuff him to that good solid radiator, and then go through the back and bring in your colleague and the Sergeant. And mind you don't get shot by Haig on your way out of the back door, man!"

When Farrell was safely tethered, Bryce pocketed his own gun and looked at the one in the drawer.

"I wonder you went to the trouble of getting a new gun to use on Jimmy – but perhaps too many people could tie this one to you. Ah well, I always prefer a feast rather than a famine where evidence is concerned. We've got enough to hang you three times over now."

Farrell didn't speak a word and his face was inscrutable. Haig and Dacre returned with Whymark.

"Sergeant, you and Yapp go through the house and make sure there's nobody else here. When you've done that, bag that gun up, Yapp ready to take back to the Yard. I'm going to make a start at looking for anything else of interest in the house.

"Dacre, Whymark, cuff Danny here to one of you, and then take him back to your station. Use one of our cars. One of you can bring the car back here when you've got him booked in. I'll come and charge him later. Remember he's a very dangerous man; don't allow him an inch, and keep him in cuffs until he's safely locked in a cell."

Farrell spoke for the first time. "I want my solicitor," he said.

Bryce thought his accent was a cultivated

attempt at Received Pronunciation, rather than natural.

"I'm sure you do," replied the DCI pleasantly. "We'll sort that out when you're safely behind bars. Not that it will help you."

When Farrell had been taken away, Bryce sat at the desk and looked through the drawers. Almost the first item he found was a thick bundle of ten-pound notes. 'Wouldn't it be nice if these are in the same sequence as the ones used to buy the pistol', he mused; and repeated the thought out loud when Haig and Yapp returned to report that the house was empty, and had no sign that anyone else lived in it.

Bryce found two ledger-type volumes in the desk, one some sort of cash book, and the other full of names, addresses, and comments. He scanned quickly through these, and put them both aside ready to take away.

"I'm going back to the Yard with these," he said. Looks like interesting reading. Might well help the local DDI to crack a few more cases in his patch, but I'll see if there's anything for us first. I'll take the remaining car.

"I want you two to go back over the house and check particularly for other weapons – he might keep one in his bedside cupboard, for instance. Any further evidence would be nice.

"When the local boys bring the other car back, just make your way back to the Yard. Lock up here – you should find some keys somewhere.

"Finally, let's have your gun, Sergeant, and I'll book it back in with mine."

Bryce unloaded both pistols, put the bullets back in the boxes, and shoved everything back in his pockets.

"A very good day, sir," said Haig.

"Yes indeed," replied Bryce. "A lot of work to be done now, tying in the various witness statements, and so on. But with what we already have, the best KC in the land won't be able to get Danny off the hook. Well done, both of you."

PETER ZANDER-HOWELL

DEATH ON A LONDON BUS

PETER ZANDER-HOWELL

June 1946

With routes all around the City and its environs, and with stops positioned at much closer intervals than tube stations, London buses were an unrivalled form of public transport, thought Sergeant Harold Parkes, as he made his way to work on one. It wasn't just the extensive network of the double-decker services that Harold valued; he had great affection for the vehicles themselves.

Like many passengers (boys and men in particular), he had the knack of safely letting go of the pole on the open platform, and jumping off whilst the bus was still moving. To Parkes, there was something pleasingly Errol Flynn-esque in accomplishing this manoeuvre without mishap. No cutlass between the teeth or swashbuckling, of course; but a nonchalant swagger after hitting the ground running was justified, he felt, and actually rather dashing in its way.

This morning, the Sergeant was riding on an experimental 'Pay-As-You-Board' London bus for the first time. RT97 had started off as a conventional red bus; but after bomb damage it had been converted to join the other vehicles in the odd little PAYB fleet. Unsuccessful on a busy Ealing route, it had been sprayed green, and was now working a Green Line Service from Romford to Aldgate.

Hearing of the trial, Parkes had made enquires at Romford bus garage to find out exactly where it was running. As the timetable had been convenient for his shift, he had caught the bus – curious to have an early look at what might be the future.

So far, he was unimpressed. The fact that the open platform was enclosed by doors when the bus was moving was not to his liking at all (although he could see this was essential from a safety point of view, given the other modifications).

Instead of roving up and down the bus collecting fares as the bus trundled along, the conductor was now permanently seated facing the closed platform. Parkes acknowledged a benefit for the conductor in this new arrangement – he no longer had to lug around his tray of tickets and a punching machine. But, for the travelling public, the Sergeant could only see problems.

If a large number of passengers all boarded at the same stop, they would effectively be trapped on the bouncing and swaying platform while the conductor took fares, gave change, and issued tickets. Parkes doubted that the conductor would be able to process an influx of boarding passengers fast enough between some of the shorter distance stops. That would mean those who wanted to get off would have to get past everyone standing on the platform. After which, yet more passengers would join those still waiting to pay from the last stop. Inconvenient to the point of being daft, he thought.

Then there was the new layout of RT97's stairs, which no longer rose from the platform and were repositioned past the conductor's seat – in amongst the lower deck seats. To the Sergeant, it was inexplicable that anyone thought seating should be sacrificed – and presumably profit at the same time – by repositioning the staircase in such a way that fewer passengers could be carried.

It didn't take long for Parkes to conclude that, if this was indeed how all London buses were to be configured, he would give the Central Line extension a try when it opened in December. The new tube station would mean a quick, two-stop journey from his home in Mile End to his police station in Liverpool Street. It would be very handy.

Parkes was disappointed with his own conclusion, but couldn't argue against it, given what he had seen this morning. He regretted that his future commute would be via the underground instead of by bus; tunnels generally being better suited to moles, and not humans, in his opinion.

The Sergeant's ruminations were ended abruptly by a woman's scream, apparently coming from the top of the stairs in the upper deck.

The screaming continued, urgent and

sustained. Parkes went to investigate.

Ernest Frampton, the bus conductor that morning, also sensed trouble and gave three sharp bursts on the bell – the signal for an emergency stop.

The driver duly applied his brakes as soon as he could, and pulled into the side of the road. Even before the bus came to a stop, the upper deck passengers started to descend in a rush, trying to get into the lower saloon.

Their intentions were thwarted by Sergeant Parkes, who by now was solidly straddling the foot of the stairs. As the first two passengers continued to descend, he put down a large black boot on the bottom step and, for good measure, raised his hand in the name of the law.

"Now then, what's all this?" he enquired of a woman in her fifties, grasping the stair rail in one hand, a basket and neatly furled umbrella in the other.

"Dead man. A dead man," she stuttered.

Following behind her, another woman confirmed this report:

"She's right, Sergeant – there's a man up there. Looks like he's bled to death."

There were now more passengers attempting to come down. Harold Parkes remained immovable, completely blocking the narrow exit. But even as he appeared to be impassively preventing evacuation of the upper deck, the Sergeant was making important calculations.

As an officer of the City of London Police, he only policed within the 'Square Mile' and not beyond. The bus had halted almost opposite Aldgate East tube station, and Parkes was pretty sure that it was about a hundred yards outside his force's jurisdiction. That meant, if there had been an offence, it must have been committed in the Metropolitan Police area. It was the Met that had to be informed; not his own colleagues in Bishopsgate which was a few hundred yards further on.

Moreover, he wasn't sure of the situation. He contemplated whether he should ascertain the facts upstairs before doing anything further, but rejected that idea. His first priority was to summon assistance. His second job – as any police officer faced with a possible murder knew – was to keep the scene and any suspects secure.

With the conductor now beside him and looking at him for guidance, the second of Harold's tasks became the first to be accomplished:

"You go back and keep those doors tight shut" he ordered Ernest Frampton. "And don't you open them under any circumstances without my say-so."

The conductor nodded.

Meanwhile, the driver, Gordon Cloot, having not received any information to explain the emergency stop, climbed out of his cab and tapped on the closed platform doors, expecting to be let in.

His colleague started to explain through a window why he wasn't opening the doors, but Sergeant Parkes interrupted. Uncoupling his whistle from its chain, he passed it through the window to the driver.

"We need help here urgently. You blow on this hard, and keep it up until a police officer arrives."

Cloot didn't need to be told twice. As an aficionado of American westerns, he was familiar with the practice of a lawman assembling a posse or creating a deputy when required. In the absence of a silver star, he was happy to accept a silver whistle instead as his mark of authority. Filling his lungs, he enthusiastically obeyed the Sergeant's orders and released a series of piercing blasts; paused, then repeated the salvo.

In no time at all a very young constable ran up to the bus. Seeing a liveried bus operative blowing a police whistle, he was about to remonstrate with the driver when he saw the Sergeant waving at him from inside the bus.

Again communicating through the window, Parkes rapidly summarised the position. He told the constable to report to the nearest police station that there may have been a murder on the bus.

"I'll run down to Leman Street. It's only a couple of hundred yards," said the constable. "I was there ten minutes ago, and the DI was in the foyer talking to the Sarge. Maybe he'll still be there."

Constable Akers ran off with all the speed and energy that come naturally to the youthful and athletic.

Mercifully for the ears of those nearby, the driver no longer had any need to blow the whistle. Almost reluctantly, he passed it back through the window.

While all this had been going on, the kerfuffle from the stairs and upper deck had grown in volume.

Disembodied shouts in London accents came down from above:

'There's a dead man up here!"

"Get a move on down there, why don't you?"

"Fer Gawd's sake lerrus orf!"

Parkes shouted back to the unseen passengers:

"I'm a police officer. I've sent for help. Have a bit of patience, please – we'll have you down as quick as we can."

The Sergeant rapidly considered. The desire of the top deck passengers to get downstairs was very understandable. From an investigation point of view, it was also preferable to enable such a transfer as soon as possible. Apart from himself, there were only four lower deck passengers – all of whom were swivelled around in their seats, riveted to his every word and movement.

Still blocking the stairs, Sergeant Parkes turned and addressed his small audience:

"You heard what they're saying upstairs.

This is a very serious situation. I want to let them come downstairs – but not until I've let you off first.

"Each of you get your ID card out ready to show me. I'll take a note of your details in case you're needed as witnesses. Then you can all go."

This exercise – which was met with relief and total co-operation – was completed inside five minutes. Next, the Sergeant instructed the conductor:

"Open the doors to let this lot off now; then shut them again sharpish."

As the platform doors closed behind the disembarking quartet, Parkes took the opportunity to also note the conductor's details and check his ID.

With his paperwork completed, the Sergeant at last moved his hefty frame from the foot of the stairs, leaving only one of his arms bridging across the exit. To the first two passengers he said:

"I'm going to let you ladies past one by one. You're to come down calmly and go and sit at the front of the bus." To the remainder of the top deck passengers, he repeated the same instructions.

Harold was surprised to see that a total of only seven passengers descended – the noise from above had suggested many more. Two women and five men obediently sat towards the front of the lower saloon. Noticeably, none shared a seat, and all distanced themselves as far as practicable from their neighbours.

For several minutes a welcome silence fell over the traumatised passengers, ruined only when a vociferous Eastender repeatedly insisted he wanted to get off the bus; then demanded he be allowed to do so.

Parkes chose to ignore the man's clamour for a while, until it became clear that his loud accusations of 'wrongfoul' arrest were reaching the ears of passing pedestrians through the open window.

Towering over the seated agitator, Sergeant Parkes warned him that interfering with a legal process was a very serious matter, and that the penalty for such conduct was a heavy one.

Silence again fell over the lower deck.

****

PC Akers returned to the bus with two men in suits, both of whom had no difficulty in matching the constable's pace. One of these, a good-looking man with brown hair neatly parted on the left, tapped on the door, and identified himself to the Sergeant and conductor via the window:

"I'm Detective Inspector Bryce, and with me is Detective Sergeant Williams."

Turning towards Constable Akers, the DI instructed him to stay outside and guard the emergency exit, and then told the bus driver that he was also to remain outside.

The conductor, mindful of Harold's earlier warning, made no move to open the bus doors until Parkes gave him a verbal prodding:

"Let them on then, man!"

Once aboard the bus, the junior Detective stepped into the lower saloon whilst the Inspector stood on the platform with Harold.

"What have we got here then, Sergeant?" asked Bryce.

Parkes gave a succinct report, explaining that he had not, as yet, been upstairs to verify the allegation of a dead man.

"Good," replied the DI. Turning to his subordinate he said:

"Nip upstairs, Williams, and take a look."

The seven remaining travellers were all watching and listening. One of the last passengers to descend the stairs, a smartly dressed businessman, had heard Bryce identify himself and called out:

"It's right enough, Inspector. There's a man dead, and some blood."

Seconds later DS Williams called down his official verification:

"Yup; a body, sir. On the very back seat. Stabbed."

"I see," acknowledged the Inspector, and began to address the lower saloon in a loud and clear voice:

"Ladies and gentlemen, you all heard that. Needless to say, this appears to be an unlawful killing. Nobody is leaving this bus until I've ascertained exactly who you are, and what you saw."

He called his Sergeant down again.

"Go into a shop or the underground station and commandeer a telephone. Call for the police surgeon to come here as soon as possible. Take the bus driver with you so he can tell his depot what's happened. Then both of you come straight back."

The conductor opened the doors again, to allow Williams to leave.

Bryce continued:

"Sergeant, I see from your insignia that you're a City officer – Bishopsgate police station?"

Parkes nodded.

"I assume you don't want to get involved any further, but it's possible we'll need to talk to you later. You may be able to corroborate what the conductor will say about who got on and off, and at what point.

"Add your details, please, to the information you've already taken from everyone downstairs."

When Parkes had done this, Bryce took the proffered pages torn from his police pocketbook and thanked the Sergeant, signalling to the conductor to let him off.

Turning to the seven restless passengers he said:

"I'm sorry about all this, but I'm sure you can see the problem. While I'm not saying at this point that one of you is responsible, it must be a serious possibility.

"I want each of you to come to me one at a time. Tell me your name, address, and the reason for your journey. If you were going to work, I want to know where your workplace is. Back up everything you say by producing your identity card. If you saw what actually happened, or indeed if you recognised the dead man, then of course you must say so."

It took a good fifteen minutes for the DI to take down everyone's details. Nobody said they recognised the deceased man, and all claimed not to have witnessed the stabbing. Two passengers thought the man had got on board at the Bow Church stop.

Just as Bryce finished collating these points, Sergeant Williams returned.

"Doctor Bloor will be here in about half an hour," he reported as he re-boarded the bus.

"Good," replied the DI. "Your next job Sergeant is to go upstairs again, and see what you can find on the deceased. Take some photographs, while you're at it. When you get down I'll tell you what's happening next."

****

Williams returned in due course and handed Bryce a wallet and an identity card.

"Gerry Gates, jeweller, of Romford," he reported. "I haven't touched him except to get at his inside pocket, but it looks as though he's taken a knife under the ribs.

"He was carrying a little strong box chained to his left wrist; all intact as far as I can tell, sir, without pulling it out to take a better look."

Bryce looked at the ID card and shared his thoughts with his Sergeant:

"Obviously, we need to interview all these people and take formal statements. We also need to search them and the bus for the weapon. All of which will take quite a bit of time. I don't see that we can reasonably keep them here without access to a telephone to contact employers or family – and without access to lavatories, for that matter.

"We'll have to get them down to a police station. It might be marginally nearer Commercial Street from here, but Leman Street is better for us. I'll stay on board to search the bus and wait for the Police Surgeon – you and Akers will escort the passengers to the station."

Bryce, already speaking in a low voice, lowered it further:

"I want them walked in a tight formation, Williams. Put the two women at the front – neither could run far or fast in their heels. Akers should walk near the kerb beside three men in the middle; and you at the rear, close behind the last two men. Both of you need to be ready to chase if anyone tries to make a run for it, so warn Akers."

The Sergeant nodded that he understood, and Bryce continued:

"When you've given them some

refreshments and nose-powdering time, start the interviews. Ask particularly where each person was seated, and what they recall about where other passengers were seated. Crucially, record where each person got on the bus."

Williams again indicated that he had grasped his orders, and Bryce turned to address the passengers, all now sitting silently.

"I appreciate this isn't convenient for any of you. Some of you will want to contact your employer or family, and some may need other facilities. But we must detain you until we have a formal statement from each of you.

"You're going to be escorted to the police station shortly. Before that, however, we also need to find the weapon which killed the man upstairs. You will all be searched before you leave the bus.

"We can do a quick pat-down for the men, and we can search your briefcases, bags and baskets. I'll confess I'm in a little difficulty with you two ladies, though."

Hearing this, the two women looked at each other across the aisle of the bus and silent communication took place. One raised her eyebrows and pointed first to herself and then to her fellow passenger. The other nodded.

The woman who had earlier been screaming now seemed to have recovered her spirits and said:

"If it would help, Inspector, we are prepared to 'pat down' each other, in your presence, of course. I can assure you we're not in cahoots, and I don't even know this lady's name, although we've seen each other on this bus route quite a few times before."

"Very helpful suggestion, that's much appreciated," said Bryce. He rapped on the window and beckoned to Akers to leave his post and come back on board.

"These ladies are going to pat each other down, under your eye, so get that done first. Then you search all the men.

"Whilst I'm taking a look upstairs, the Sergeant here will check all your hand luggage. We will also collect each of your tickets, and mark them to show ownership."

Akers started the search procedure, fortunate that all seven were now quite docile. The Constable found nothing incriminating and Williams the same – there was nothing untoward in anything the passengers were carrying.

Returning from his trip to the top deck, Bryce made his announcement:

"The Sergeant and Constable will walk down to the police station with you. It's only two or three hundred yards. There, you will be given access to a telephone. We will also find you some refreshment.

"We've established that the victim upstairs is Gerry Gates. If any of you know him; or if you've heard of him, please say so when you are interviewed. I may see you at the police station, but provisionally, after each of you has made your statement, you may go."

Williams and Akers organised the passengers as instructed, and Bryce noted with approval that Williams told each of the five men precisely where they were to stand, rather than letting them arrange themselves into the middle and back rows. He felt it wouldn't be long before his subordinate got a well-earned promotion.

Assembled, the little crocodile started walking towards Leman Street police station, leaving Bryce with the driver still cooling his heels outside, and the conductor still on board.

"I'll need a statement from you as well," said the DI to Frampton. "You might like to be thinking about that. The dead man is quite distinctive – about sixty years old, bald, and wearing a dark suit with a very faint pinstripe. If you can say where he got on – and where each of the others got on – that would help. Although I suppose their tickets will confirm that."

"I think he got on at Bow Church sir," said the conductor. "I can't say for sure about the others – although the two ladies got on at the start. I've seen them before. But the tickets won't give you the exact stop – the fares are same from more than one bus stop. What we call fare stages is where the prices change."

"Yes, I see. What about people getting off?"

"Nobody got off, from upstairs or down, after Stratford, sir. That's definite. We don't stop at all the red bus stops, of course."

"Very helpful. Just show me how to operate these doors please, and then you can go and join your driver while I search the bus."

The DI shut the doors behind the conductor, and went upstairs to search for a knife. Like his Sergeant, he avoided touching the victim, but noted what Williams had reported – the small black case chained to the Gates's left wrist. There was no sign of a weapon anywhere on the top deck.

A search of the downstairs was similarly fruitless.

Bryce sat down in the conductor's seat, and thought hard. Something was odd. He had discovered long ago that clearing his mind of a problem, and thinking of something completely different for a few minutes, sometimes brought enlightenment.

Being familiar with RT buses, as every Londoner was, he spent a few minutes assessing this adapted one. He had never seen a Pay-As-You-Board vehicle before, and while noting the way the platform and stairs had been rearranged, he thought that the new design would not find favour with many – if any – people. The thought of elderly or disabled users, or those with small children, rocking about on the platform while they waited to pay, instead of being safely seated, struck him as a backwards step.

After a few minutes, he allowed his brain to revert to considering the absence of a weapon. A knife with a blade sufficiently long to stab a man could not have been missed in the body searches. Even a folding knife would still be of a substantial size.

Was it feasible that the man had received a fatal wound elsewhere, and then somehow managed to board the bus, pay his fare, and climb the stairs to the upper deck, only to expire there?

His own answer to this question was 'ridiculous!' but he nevertheless resolved to ask the same of the police surgeon when he arrived.

Realising that the only places he hadn't looked were on the body itself, and immediately beneath it, he went back up the stairs to make a check.

The man was slumped, leaning partly against the back of the seat and partly against the adjacent window. Bryce lifted first his left arm – the one with the chain attached – and then the right. This arm was stiff and unbending. Bryce found that something rigid had been pushed into the sleeve of the man's suit. Carefully edging this out, he found the missing weapon – a switchblade. Eying it with the distaste endemic among policemen, he put it down on the seat in front.

It occurred to him that the dead man's ticket hadn't been with his wallet and papers. He felt in the jacket pockets without success and, with difficulty, in the trousers. The ticket was in a pocket.

The sound of banging on the bus door took him downstairs again. A wavy-haired man in his thirties, wearing a tweed jacket and brogues, stood at the door, the medical bag in his hand showing his credentials. Not that Bryce needed that clue, as he knew Dr Bloor well.

The DI opened the doors to admit the police surgeon.

"Good morning, Jonathan."

"Good morning to you too, Philip," came the warm reply. "And yours will be better than mine, I guarantee. I've had to leave a surgery full of patients and I can tell already that this is one of those days when I shan't get my lunch before bedtime!"

"I have days like that myself, Jonathan. At least your wife will have something for you when you eventually get home," Bryce shot back at his friend with a smile.

"All true, Philip, all true. And if you would only make yourself more agreeable to all the rather nice girls that Rebecca tries to put your way, your supper could be waiting for you too, old chap."

Bryce smiled and nodded at his friend, but made no comment. He knew what Bloor said was absolutely correct – his wife had tried repeatedly to introduce him to her charming and suitable friends. But none had held a candle to Anne – his fiancée killed in the war – and he had made no effort to see any of the disappointed girls again.

"Where is he, then?" asked the medic looking around the lower deck.

Bryce indicated with his thumb.

"Can I move him around?" called Bloor, as he disappeared up the stairs.

"Yes," replied Bryce, "and you'll see the presumed weapon on the seat in front of him.

"I don't expect much from you this time, Jonathan. When I couldn't find the weapon, I was going to ask if he could have been stabbed elsewhere and walked onto the bus afterwards – not that it seemed very likely. But then I found the knife hidden up his own sleeve.

"So now all I need is a clear statement from you to say that the wound couldn't have been self-inflicted, and that even if it was, he couldn't possibly have folded the knife afterwards, and shoved it away up his sleeve. A scenario which, to a layman like me, seems even more improbable than the other.

"But you know what defence counsel are like, Jonathan. They want chapter and verse from a certified expert – or even from some quack like you – before they'll accept the glaringly obvious!"

Bloor laughed loudly. It was testament to their strong friendship that the two could parry in this good-humoured way. The doctor was quick with his riposte:

"I defer to your knowledge of counsels' habits, Philip – being a member of that closed shop of overpaid actors yourself!"

His own laughter abated, Bryce, having followed the doctor up the stairs, eyed the weapon again.

"I'll get a bag for that in a minute," he said.

The doctor leaned over the dead man. He used a sharp blade of his own to cut away a lower portion of the victim's shirt, to get a better view.

"I'll need to get him on the slab to be a hundred percent sure, Philip. But first thoughts are that the heart was pierced by a single blow. That switchblade seems to have a longer blade than some – it would have the reach to do the job.

"There is no question that he was attacked. He could never have stabbed himself. As you well know!"

Dr Bloor straightened up. "Probably easiest to get him to the mortuary at the London. Only a few hundred yards, and doing an autopsy there is rather more congenial than in the public morgue."

"All right, Jonathan, I'll arrange that. Do you want to inform the coroner, or shall I?"

"You, please. I'll get back to see any of my patients who are still waiting, and then go straight along to the London and start the PM. Say about noon. Will you attend, or will you send somebody?"

"I may come myself – depends on what I find at the station. And someone will have to come to take charge of that case," he said, gesturing towards the little black box chained to the victim's wrist.

At just the right moment, PC Akers returned. He jovially saluted the doctor who was just getting off the bus.

"Sergeant Williams has the interviews under way, sir," he said to the DI. "He sent me back to ask is there's anything I can do?"

"There is, Akers. Two things, actually. First, pop into that clothes shop over there, and ask them for a couple of carrier bags so I can carry this knife away. I'd like to double-wrap it.

"When you come back, stay here and guard the bus until the body's taken off. Then travel in the back of the ambulance to the London Hospital and don't leave the deceased until I tell you otherwise." Bryce explained about the black box chained to the victim's wrist, stressing that he wanted no chances taken with it.

"You two gentlemen," he said to the bus crew standing nearby, "I don't mind if you take a seat with this officer downstairs when he comes back, but neither you nor anyone else except the ambulance men is to go upstairs.

"When the body is removed, you can have your bus back. There's a bit of blood upstairs, so I guess it'll need cleaning before going back into service. I'm sorry your day has been disrupted."

"No worries, guv," said Ernest Frampton. "Bit of an experience in its way, and none of it's ruined our day as much as it has that poor blighter's upstairs."

"Ain't that the truth," agreed Gordon Cloot.

****

With the knife carefully double-bagged,

Bryce made his way back to his office in Leman Street. The history of the Leman Street and Commercial Street stations was most interesting to the DI, and something he had thought about more than once since taking up his new post after his demob. These two stations had been the principal bases for the detectives investigating the cases known as the 'Whitechapel Murders'.

Despite – according to the then Metropolitan Police Commissioner – over a hundred and forty extra plain clothes officers being deployed in the area (and detectives from the City force as well), the murderer of possibly eleven women was never identified.

Bryce wondered where this remarkable number of plain clothes men had come from, and of what calibre they might have been. He hoped that he and DS Williams would have more success in such an investigation in 1946, than their predecessors had managed between 1888 and 1891.

Entering the station, Bryce went in search of his Sergeant, and found him talking to one of the passengers in an interview room. Joining his boss outside the room, Williams told him:

"Five down, two to go, sir, but nothing remarkable to report from anyone so far."

Bryce left Williams to finish the interview himself, and returned to his own office to telephone the London Hospital and the Coroner's office.

This done, the DI went in search of the two remaining witnesses. He found the two women chatting to each other over cups of tea. It transpired that they had volunteered to go last, since they were in no particular hurry.

"Sergeant Williams will see you shortly, ladies – so this isn't your formal interview. But you said you were fairly regular passengers on that bus. As I told you all earlier, the man's name seems to be Gerry Gates, and he was probably a jeweller. Just think again, please. Does that name ring any bells? Or have you seen him before – on the bus or anywhere?"

Both women shook their heads. The older of the pair, Constance Norlake, said that she was sitting in the front left-hand seat, and saw the victim waiting at the Bow Church stop.

"I noticed him because he was so nattily dressed, and clutching this little black case, and I could see a bit of chain attached to it. Now you've said he was a jeweller, I suppose that means he was carrying valuables."

Laura Unwin, who had been sitting in the right-hand front seat, had also seen him waiting, although she hadn't noticed the case.

Both women thought that several others had also been waiting at Bow Church, although neither could describe anyone there, nor indeed could they even say if any had joined the same service – Bow Church being a stop on several routes.

In fact, neither woman had even realised that the man had come up to the top deck. Mrs Unwin, rising ready to get off at the next (Aldgate) stop, saw him slumped and bloodied at the back as she went to go down the stairs. It was she who had screamed.

Sergeant Williams came into the room to collect his next interviewee. Bryce told him that the women had noticed the man at Bow, and emphasised that that point needed to be included.

"You've been very patient, ladies, thank you," he said. "Sergeant, when you've finished, come along to my office and bring all the tickets as well as the statements with you."

****

Bryce had hardly reached his office when his telephone rang. It was his immediate superior – the Divisional Detective Inspector.

"The Leman Street custody sergeant called me, on your instructions, I gather. He told me that you'd 'gone for a run up the road'. Possible murder on a bus, is it? What's the situation? Do you need support? Or do we need to ask for help from the Yard?"

Bryce gave his boss a précis of events.

"I'm confident that Sergeant Williams and I can handle this, sir," he said. "The deceased had a case locked to his wrist, which presumably contains valuables – it seems he was a jeweller by trade – but there was no attempt to take it. I don't think this was a robbery. It looks more like a professional killing – although I have to admit it seems a very odd place to choose."

The DDI was a good judge of men and immediately agreed the matter should be left to Bryce. Although the DI had only been attached to 'H' Division a few months ago, he had already created a very favourable impression on his superior.

A few minutes after Bryce put his telephone down, Williams arrived, carrying a sheaf of papers and the seven tickets. He laid these on the desk, and sat down at the DI's invitation.

Bryce relayed to his Sergeant where the weapon had been found. He also reported the conductor's comment about no-one leaving the bus after Stratford – which meant that if Gates was killed on the bus, the murderer must be one of the seven top deck passengers.

"I've let the conductor go without taking a formal statement, but we may well have to see him again to get that point confirmed in writing.

"What have you extracted from our seven suspects?"

"Well, sir, not a lot emerged from the interviews. No-one, so they say, even noticed Gates come upstairs. They all reckon they were facing forward the whole time – which is feasible, I suppose – if he got on last and went straight to the very back seat, of course. As you heard, both women saw him waiting at Bow, but even they didn't know he'd definitely got onto their bus.

"I've drawn a little plan of the upper deck, showing where people said they were sitting."

Williams pushed the sketch across the table, and Bryce looked at it closely.

"Let's examine the tickets, and see if we can draw any conclusions from those. We need to bear in mind that, as the conductor told me, one can travel from different stops for the same fare." He produced the ticket he had taken from the dead man's pocket and added it to the others.

Unfortunately, the little collection produced limited information. Mrs Unwin and Mrs Norlake had boarded in Romford, at the start of the bus's journey. Mr Ashmore after that, at Gidea Park according to his statement, and Mr Earl said he got on at Ilford.

That left Messrs Peters, Dent, and Pratt. Their three tickets, plus Gates's own, all showed the same fare.

Peters could have boarded a stop or two before Gates; and Dent and Pratt could have boarded a stop or so later. However, the likelihood was that all four had boarded at Bow. Williams, looking through the statements, confirmed that these three witnesses all said they had boarded at Bow.

Bryce also quickly scanned the statements of the Bow stop witnesses.

"Hmmm, as you say. None of those three said they'd even noticed Gates while they were waiting. Yet Mrs Unwin said he looked distinctive, and Mrs Norlake noticed him too. While I suppose Peters and Co might have had their noses in the morning papers or something, it seems a bit odd that not one of the three of them noticed Gates. Although in fairness, neither woman particularly noticed the other three men who boarded with Gates.

"When I spoke to the DDI just now, I told him I didn't think this was a botched robbery. I think this is most likely a job done to order. Any view yourself, Williams?"

"I don't know, sir. Surely there must be far easier places to kill the man?"

"Yes, indeed. But my tentative theory is this: having decided to stab Gates on the bus, the killer might normally have expected to run straight down the stairs, jump off, and disappear. But that wouldn't be possible on this specific bus with its enclosed platform.

"Alternatively, and I concede perhaps more likely, he might never have intended to kill Gates on the bus, but simply intended to follow Gates to wherever he was going, do the deed, and escape in a crowd.

"But anyway, when he gets upstairs, he sees Gates sitting alone at the back, and only a handful of other passengers, all facing forwards."

"So, admittedly showing remarkable sangfroid, he decides to do the hit regardless, realising that if he makes it quick his action won't be seen. Then, he coolly sits down elsewhere. The other passengers are all near the front of the bus. Nobody sees him do it. Nobody sees him move forwards afterwards.

"He still hopes to be able to get off before his crime is discovered, of course."

Sergeant Williams looked rather sceptical.

"Blimey, sir, that would take someone with almost unbelievable nerve! I'm not saying you're wrong, of course, but…"

"I know," replied the DI. "But if I'm right, and this was a professional killing, surely anyone with that occupation must automatically have nerves of steel?"

Williams remained doubtful.

"Wouldn't an attempted robbery be more likely, sir? Maybe the robber found out too late that the box was chained to the man."

"Possible, I agree," said Bryce. "However, let's work on my theory for a minute.

"There is no evidence that Gates was a regular on this route. Therefore, nobody intending to kill him could have boarded at an earlier stop and know that he would be getting on at Bow. Equally, nobody could get on at a later stop and know for sure that Gates would already be on the bus.

"My conclusion is that the killer must be one of those who boarded the bus at the same time as Gates – Peters, Pratt or Dent."

"I can go along with that, sir, but whoever

it was could have stabbed Gates in Bow, before ever getting on the bus. That's the bit that makes no sense at all to me. It must be just as easy to disappear in Bow – or elsewhere in the city – and far easier than on a Green Line bus!"

"I agree. What we have isn't logically arranged at all from our point of view, and I can't imagine why Gates wasn't attacked in Bow. But as I see things, we already have our murderer right here – we just need to identify him.

"Do a records check on our witnesses. Get onto the Yard now, and see what they might have. Just to be sure, ask about all seven as well as Frampton the conductor – but prioritise our three most likely candidates.

"When you've done that, ring the custody sergeant at Bow. Ask him if he has ever come across Peters, Dent, or Pratt – Gates too while you're at it. If he hasn't, ask him to make enquiries among other officers.

"Finally, check the knife for prints. He indicated the bag on a little table in the corner of the room. Zero chance of finding any, of course, even if my theory about a professional is wrong.

"I'm going along to the London Hospital to observe the PM."

****

Doctor Bloor was just getting ready to start the autopsy when Bryce arrived. Thanking Constable Akers for his assistance, Bryce told him to take a quick break and then go back to the police station.

The mortuary attendant began to remove Gates's clothes, but was hampered in doing this by the presence of the case and chain. William Hopkin had spent many years performing mortuary duties, and was inclined to demonstrate gallows humour if he thought the pathologist wouldn't object. Sucking air noisily through his teeth he shook his head and said:

"Well, we do have choices, which is always a nice position to be in, I say. We could waste a lot of time finding some bolt cutters or a hacksaw for the chain. Or you could cut his hand off at the wrist, doc."

Hopkin added:

"Or we could just see if he has the key secreted on his person somewhere."

The latter course obviously being his intention from the outset, Hopkin had already started feeling around the body, first to ascertain if there was a body belt. When that proved negative, he tried for an anklet, but failed again. Finally, he opened the top few shirt buttons. "Third time lucky," he announced, revealing a second chain around the dead man's neck, from which hung the two keys.

Bloor gently lifted the man's head, and the attendant reached behind, unhooked the clip on the chain to release it, and handed the length to Bryce.

"I can't think it's ever a good idea to actually carry the key in these circumstances, but people do seem to do this," said Bryce. "Perhaps they think that in a dire situation, it's preferable to be able to say 'here's the key'".

He inserted the smaller key into the lock on Gates's wrist, and released the box. "All yours now, Billy," he said to the attendant, who recommenced his undressing operation.

Bryce debated whether to open the case immediately, or wait until he was back at the station. Curiosity won. Putting the case down on a side table, he used the second key to unlock it. Lifting the lid of the little box, he peered inside. Nestling amongst some scrunched up cloth – which might have been two or three handkerchiefs – was a royal blue velvet bag, a drawstring pulled tight at its neck.

Walking over to where various autopsy equipment was stored, Bryce selected a small enamel kidney dish. Cutting a short length of gauze from a roll, he used that to line the bowl. Opening the drawstring, he gently tipped the contents of the bag into the bowl, and found himself looking at fifty or so small stones. Some were clear like little bits of crystal; others had tinges of yellow or pink; three were black. All were octahedral or cubic in shape.

Bryce knew just enough about precious stones to realise that these were uncut diamonds. He showed them to the doctor and attendant, before tipping them back into their velvet pouch, and locking it in the case again.

He had no idea of their value, but he fixed the chain to his own wrist, and fastened the neck chain and key around his own neck.

Rejoining Bloor and Hopkin, he stood to one side and watched as the men performed their clinical duties. This took some time, and the three men carried on a casual conversation as the work was done.

Some pathologists employed a secretary, and dictated their findings as they went along. Bloor preferred not to have a woman in the room, and although he occasionally made a note during a PM, generally he relied on his elephantine memory to produce a report afterwards.

"Well, Philip," he said eventually, "as we thought at the scene, there was one single blow. Went straight into the heart. Unconsciousness would have supervened within seconds. Death would have occurred within a minute or so. Some bleeding, as you saw, but really not that much."

"Anyway, I can see you want to get away with the loot. I'll check the rest of him for disease, poisons, etc. and let you have the results as soon as I can."

Bryce thanked the men. Making his way to the exit he briefly considered either asking for a police car to come and collect him, or alternatively hailing a taxi. Eventually deciding to do neither, he left the hospital, and walked the half-mile back to

Leman Street, arriving without incident.

Without explaining his reason for asking, the DI enquired whether the station possessed a safe. Receiving a 'no, sir' response, Bryce took the box up to his office, where he removed the chain from his wrist and locked the little case in his desk drawer. Adding his desk key to the two already on the chain around his neck, he felt he had done as much as possible to secure the stones.

Feeling hungry, Bryce decided it was time for lunch and left the station again, arriving a few minutes later at a favourite café on the Whitechapel Road. He always ate as well as possible at lunch times. It was one less thing to bother with in the evening, when he returned home tired to his bachelor flat.

A plate of liver and onions left him feeling satisfied and with barely enough room for the rice pudding he had ordered. His 'inner man' appeased, he left a generous tip for the waitress who had served him and strolled back to his office.

****

Still concerned about the diamonds, Bryce picked up the telephone and asked to be connected to Detective Inspector Jesty at Holborn. Jesty was at his desk and delighted to hear from his old acquaintance. After a couple of minutes of chat, Bryce got down to the purpose of his call:

"I need an introduction to a good diamond expert, George," he said. "And before you make an asinine comment about valuations for my non-existent private hoard, what I need is an honest and reliable man to assess – and perhaps even identify – some seized property. Can you recommend someone?"

"Certainly can," replied Jesty. "Nathan Morris, of Morris and Morris, 6b Greville Street. I've had several dealings with him about thefts from private collections. It was Morris who helped when Lady Heysham's jewels were lifted and then re-cut. He's your man – you'll get your valuation right enough; and if he knows anything else that's useful, you'll get that too.

"I'll give him a call to tell him you're coming if you like, Philip?"

"If you would, please, George. Any time this afternoon, if that suits him."

"I'll call you in a few minutes."

True to his word, Jesty soon rang back to say that Mr Morris would expect a visit at three o'clock, but that punctuality wasn't crucial. Bryce thanked his friend and replaced the receiver.

Deciding he should go and see how his Sergeant was getting on next, he was pleased when a tap on his door turned out to be Williams, wanting to share the fruits of his searches.

"There were no police records on any of the seven passengers or the conductor, sir, and nobody at Bow had ever heard of Pratt, Peters, or Dent."

"That's a disappointment," said Bryce, his face and voice both puzzled. He had felt sure there would be something in the records on one of the three.

"One of the detectives at Bow had come across the victim during the war," continued Williams. "He was associated with a bunch of undesirables – black market connections mostly, with a sideline in theft – but Gates was never arrested, let alone charged with any offence. Always on the periphery.

"And there was absolutely no trace of a fingerprint on the knife, sir."

"All very unfortunate," said Bryce. "For my theory to hold good, one of those three men who got on at Bow Church with Gates, should have come to our attention before. Even professional assassins must start off as minor villains, surely?"

Sergeant Williams acknowledged that might well be true, but didn't like to say that in the absence of any 'previous' maybe the assassin theory was incorrect, after all; and that what they had was a robbery gone wrong.

The DI, aware of – but for the moment ignoring – his Sergeant's doubts, produced the little black case and unlocked it. Removing the blue velvet bag before passing the empty box to Williams:

"I'll keep the pouch here; you take this and check for prints, inside as well as out. When you're done, bring the box and a camera back up here – we'll take a photograph of the contents before we go to Hatton Garden to see a diamond merchant."

****

Williams returned as instructed with the case, now dusty with fingerprint powder, together with the camera.

Bryce had cleared a space on his desk. He took the gemstone bag from his drawer and opened it, carefully spreading one row of the contents out alongside a twelve-inch ruler, as it had occurred to him that photographing the stones without some sort of perspective was not ideal. Williams, who had also never seen uncut diamonds before, found himself to be rather underwhelmed by them as he operated the camera.

Several photographs later, Bryce had re-bagged and re-boxed the stones, chaining the locked box to his arm once more. The detectives went downstairs and climbed into the police car.

"Greville Street, Holborn is our destination, Williams. Let's see if we can find out the value of these stones. Also – and this a long shot – whether they're identifiable as having been stolen."

The lack of any incriminating police record for any one of the three likeliest suspects was bothering Bryce.

"It occurs to me that my theory about Peters Dent and Pratt would work if our murderer has used other names in the past. In other words, we might have records, but we don't know the name they are under."

Williams was silent for a minute, concentrating on the traffic around Ludgate Circus. He thought that a theory was well and good, but if the facts contradicted the theory, it was time to change tack. Turning into Fleet Street, he said:

"But we've got their ID cards, sir. We have to accept those as their real names, surely?"

"No. Not in this case. We may have something more, Sergeant. Thinking back to the statements, it appeared to me that each person wrote out their own, rather than you writing to their dictation?"

"That's right. I usually find that's easier – providing the witness can write, of course. And all these were pretty good."

"Excellent. The next step is to dust each of the three key statements for prints, and get them all over to the Yard."

"If you're right, sir, that would mean someone's identity card is a forgery. But I'll tell you now I couldn't pick out whose, if that really is the case. They all looked genuine to me."

"We'll see. Get the prints as soon as we get back, please."

Williams turned into Greville Street, and found a parking space outside number 6b. There was no glass in the door, and no windows on the ground floor. The only sign that this was a place of business was a tiny brass plaque discreetly identifying Morris and Morris, Ltd.

"They don't go out of their way to attract casual customers," remarked Williams.

"No indeed; I imagine business is done exclusively between dealers or merchants or whatever they're called," replied Bryce, pushing the polished brass bell. He noted a spy hole in the door, and deliberately aligned his face with it.

Within seconds, the door opened, and a burly uniformed man asked for their names. Apparently satisfied, he invited the officers in, locking the door again behind them.

The detectives found themselves in a large but very functional hallway. Green and cream 'Chrysanthemum' wallpaper ranged above and below the dado rails, whilst black and white tiles defined the floor. The entry was striking for its impressive proportions – and also the complete absence of pictures, mirrors, or furniture of any sort, even though there was ample space. The balustrade of the curved staircase ahead of them, however, wouldn't have been out of place in the stateliest of stately homes.

"Mr Nathan is expecting you," intoned the doorkeeper. "This way, gentlemen, if you please."

The detectives followed him up the beautiful staircase. He tapped on a door a few yards along the landing, and opened it without waiting for a response.

"Inspector Bryce and Sergeant Williams, sir."

This room was furnished in a manner in

keeping with its architecture. Here the walls were hung with mostly oil portraits, and the furniture was Chippendale and Hepplewhite.

From the far side of the room, a short white-haired man of perhaps seventy rose from his desk (although Bryce thought he might just as easily have stepped out of one of the portraits – his resemblance to at least three of the subjects being so strong). Dressed in a suit which could only have been made in Savile Row, Mr Morris was the epitome of the word 'distinguished'.

"Welcome, gentlemen, do please take a seat," said the diamond dealer, shaking hands with both officers.

"Mr Jesty and I get on very well, but it's always nice to meet some fresh faces. When he telephoned, he gave me something of your background, Mr Bryce. He seems to think that you'll be the Metropolitan Police Commissioner one day. And I know him well enough to know that he wasn't joking! He tells me that you are also a barrister.

"Anyway, can I offer you some refreshment? Tea?"

This was accepted, and Morris gave the order to his doorman, who appeared to be some sort of general factotum within the Morris organisation.

"Do sit down, gentlemen and, if you can spare the time, let us talk about any subject under the sun, while we await the tea."

"Well, sir," began Bryce, "first I must tell you that George Jesty's forecast is way out. It's true that I'm a barrister, but I'm short of certain attributes necessary for reaching the top of the 'greasy pole'. For a start, I lack tact and diplomacy. I'm too outspoken – especially when I think some senior officer is talking through his hat."

Williams, sitting quietly, was aware that his boss wasn't afraid to say what he thought to senior people. But although he had been working with him for several months, he had not been aware that the DI was a lawyer.

"Ah well, time will tell," laughed Morris.

"As you've discovered my undercover profession, as it were," said Bryce, "you'll realise that I must have spent a lot of time around the Inns of Court. Pre-war, of course. But although they're only yards from here, I'm ashamed to say that I've never been in Hatton Garden. I think we're both fascinated as to how you and your fellow merchants operate. I expected a shop, with glittering displays in the window."

Morris laughed. "There are places like that around here, of course, and I do business with some of them. But I, and a number of other merchants, don't do any retail trade ourselves at all. We deal with each other; and with others overseas – particularly in the Low Countries. We also buy from De Beers, of course."

"If you don't mind my asking, sir, is it true that people walk along the streets here carrying valuable diamonds in their pockets, just wrapped in a little twist of paper? And that trading is all based on a man's word, rather than on written contracts?"

Morris laughed. "Both are absolutely true, Sergeant, although most outsiders steadfastly refuse to believe it.

"It's also true that some dealers and their couriers prefer not to use a pocket. I know of one who likes to carry a string shopping bag – exactly like so many other shoppers out and about.

"The contents of his bag are very visible through the mesh, of course. His diamonds however, are invisible within the false bottom of the Vim container; or the carefully adapted sardine tin. Who would suspect, as he casually strolls to his destination, that today he is carrying a fortune in a tea packet?"

"Hidden in plain sight," said Bryce, "clever."

The diamond dealer nodded. "In the fifty years I've been in the business, I don't think there has been a single successful robbery in the Garden.

"As for your second question, Sergeant – someone reneging on a deal," Morris moved his head slowly from side to side, "they'd be completely finished in the City. So that doesn't happen either.

"Ah, here's our tea."

When the cups had been filled, and the three men were settled again, Bryce said:

"You're impressively incurious, sir. You can

see I have a case attached to my arm, but after you saw it in the first seconds, I'm pretty sure your eye hasn't even glanced at it again."

"Common politeness, mostly," smiled Morris. "But, as I've just told the Sergeant here, people wander around these parts with thousands of pounds worth of diamonds. Whatever you have brought in your case is almost certainly nothing out of the ordinary here!"

"Touché," said Bryce with a laugh. "Well, I'd still like to show you what I've got – even if it is small beer compared to what you're used to, Mr Morris. Of course, it could all be bits of stone with no value at all; but I do need to know one way or the other."

He extricated the keys from his neck and set about releasing the case. Once unlocked, he passed the velvet bag across the table.

In place of the blotting pad which most office desks would have, the dealer had a large sheet of black velvet. Undoing the bag, he gently tipped out the contents.

Williams leaned forward a little to see if the stones looked any better than they had in Bryce's office. They didn't. He decided he wouldn't be at all surprised to learn they were worthless.

Morris sat silently regarding the array on the velvet before him for two full minutes before producing a loupe. Still without speaking, he picked up a stone and examined it closely, turning it as he did so. He repeated this exercise for a further twelve stones whilst Bryce and Williams took the opportunity to drink some more of the excellent tea.

The dealer put down the loupe, took a sip of tea himself, and leaned back in his chair.

"These stones are all rough diamonds. The sizes vary, but all are somewhere between three and fifteen carats. I don't know if you are aware of this, but comparatively few rough diamonds are actually suitable for cutting and polishing – those that aren't have uses in industry.

"I can tell you that every one of these is suitable for cutting. Generally, although not always, the coloured stones have less value than the white, but even the coloured ones here are good. At least three of the white diamonds are of first-class quality.

"I should need to take a more detailed inventory, but in this uncut form, I should say this collection, as it stands, is likely to be worth between seven and nine thousand pounds on the open market. Carat for carat, a cut and polished diamond is worth perhaps eight times that of a rough stone. Obviously, weight is lost in the cutting, so the finished weight here will be a lot less than the total weight now. And the skill of the cutter has to be paid for. But if these went to a top cutter in Antwerp, they would ultimately sell for at least thirty thousand pounds."

Seeing both officers almost goggling at him, Morris laughed.

"Yes," he said. "These curious-looking lumps, some like pebbles, and others like bits of rock crystal or chunks off a beer bottle, are worth quite a lot of money.

"A sizeable, well-cut diamond is a thing of great beauty, gentlemen. But for me, these crude lumps have almost the same attraction. The process by which nature creates something so extraordinary is as fascinating as any finished and mounted stone.

"I imagine the next question you have in your mind is this," he continued "where might they have come from? I assume that these were found on some person who is not an accredited dealer?"

"The man's name is Gerry Gates," supplied Bryce. "Allegedly a jeweller. He's been murdered, incidentally, so we can't ask him any questions."

"I've never heard the name," said Morris. "And a retail jeweller would never hold this quantity of merchandise. Indeed, very few, if any, would have rough stones at all.

So, I think there are two possibilities here – both likely to be illegal.

"I know of no theft of uncut diamonds of this quantity or quality, and I should certainly have heard if there had been such a theft. As I mentioned earlier, I'm not aware of any robbery in the last fifty years.

"However, it's just possible this could be a collection of stones which have been taken one or two at a time, probably from different dealers or cutters, over a very long period.

"Alternatively, they could have been smuggled. You may know that the international supply of diamonds is almost exclusively controlled by one corporation. But despite strict controls, smuggling does occur. It would be possible to get rough diamonds in that way – but these were not sourced from the same mine. And for quality such as these, and in such quantity, I just don't know.

"I'm sorry I can't be more specific."

"You've been most helpful, sir. You've given us an idea of value, and you've more-or-less confirmed that it's very unlikely that our man was in possession of the stones legally. Thank you."

"One final point, sir. I'm not particularly keen to keep these stones – especially now I know their value. At some point, unless a legitimate owner comes forward, a magistrate will almost certainly make a decision under the Police Property Act, and direct that the goods may be sold. Would you be able to keep them in your safe or strong room, until it's decided what to do with them? I'm afraid I can't guarantee that you would get to handle any sale – that wouldn't be my decision."

"I'm happy to help, Mr Bryce. I shall need to make an inventory, so that I can give you a receipt." He lifted one of the two telephones on his desk and pressed a switch. "Mrs Dunkley, come in please."

Within seconds, a slim and smartly-dressed lady entered carrying a shorthand pad and pencil.

"Take some notes, please," instructed Morris.

Producing a tiny set of scales, Morris replaced the loupe in his eye and picked up a stone. This he described to the secretary – its weight, colour, and quality, noting any flaws at the same time. Placing that stone back in the bag, he selected another, and repeated the process.

Cataloguing the contents of the bag took nearly half an hour, but Bryce and Williams sat fascinated throughout. Both realised that they were watching a demonstration from a top expert in his field.

"Mrs Dunkley will just get that typed up. I'll sign it to acknowledge receipt, and the stones can go in my safe."

The secretary was clearly also an expert in her field, as she was back in very few minutes. Morris scanned her inventory and thanked her. She left the room, having not spoken at all.

The dealer signed the top copy, checked that his signature had come through the carbon, then handed the original to Bryce. With his back to his visitors, Morris opened his safe; casually dropped the little bag onto a tray inside, and spun the dials to re-lock it.

The two officers had risen as the dealer had, and Bryce thanked him again. After a second round of handshaking Morris escorted the officers downstairs himself, the factotum unlocking the door and letting them out.

"What did you think about that?" asked Bryce, as they drove back up Ludgate Hill.

"If you hadn't told me what they were earlier, sir I'd have thought you'd gone scavenging on a beach and picked up some odd pebbles. But it confirms what you already thought – that Gates was mixed up in some racket."

"Yes. It makes me even more sure that he was killed in some underworld falling-out.

"And a possible reason why he wasn't killed in Bow has just occurred to me. The two females on the bus – I don't suppose you got telephone numbers for either of them?"

"No, sir, neither has a telephone at home. But I know where each of them works, and I dare say they could be contacted there. I'll get you the numbers as soon as we arrive."

"Excellent. When you've done that, you start lifting the fingerprints off the statements, Sergeant, and take them immediately to the Yard yourself, as well as the prints from the box.

****

Back in his office Bryce picked up the telephone.

First, he called the company employing Mrs Norlake. Explaining who he was, he asked to speak to her. It seemed she worked as a secretary in a firm of shipping agents. She quickly came on the line.

"Good afternoon, Mrs Norlake, this is Inspector Bryce. I'm sorry to trouble you again so soon, but I have a supplementary question."

Within a few minutes he was calling Mrs Unwin. She had a similar role, this time in a firm of stockbrokers. To her he posed the same question.

Putting the telephone down, Bryce smiled in satisfaction and picked up the telephone one last time. This time he spoke to the desk sergeant downstairs.

"Gates, you've got a copy of the most recent A to Z, haven't you? Yes, 1939. Just locate Trafford Road, E3, for me please. I'll wait.

"Okay, what about Finter Street, also E3?

"Finally, Candle Street, E1?

"Thank you, Sergeant, as I expected."

Bryce decided to do a belt-and-braces check of the information the desk sergeant had given him. He left the station, and wandered up to the Whitechapel Road, looking for a black cab. Two passed quickly, both with passengers. He successfully hailed a third, and climbed in. Showing his warrant card to the driver, he announced:

"Don't drive anywhere – I'll pay you for staying put. I just want some information. You've done 'the knowledge', which I guess must be about the toughest memory test in the world."

"You got that right, guv," said the driver. "Took me nearly four years to learn, an' then when I'd just passed the war broke out. I was too old to be called up, though, so I've kept me 'and in. Whad'ya wanna know?"

"I'll give you three street names, all in East London, and I want you to tell me what you can about them.

"First, Candle Street, E1."

"Well, tha's just beside the Regent's Canal, just off Ben Jonson Road in Mile End, guv."

"Excellent. What about Finter Street, E3?"

The driver hesitated, then shook his head.

"Sorry guv, I can't place that one."

"All right, last one – Trafford Road, also E3?"

The driver now looked upset.

"Never heard of that one neither," he said. "'Ere, are you 'avin' me on?"

"Not at all," said Bryce. "I didn't think those last two existed, but I just wanted to check with someone who would know for sure, and be up to date.

"Thank you very much," he added, passing some money forwards to the driver as he got out of the taxi.

The cabbie, checking the coins in his palm, called out after Bryce:

"That's what I call 'andsome, guvnor! Much obliged!" He drove off, pleased with his tip and the fact that his 'knowledge' was good.

****

Bryce returned to his office and spent the next hour preparing papers for a court appearance in another case.

At six thirty-five the telephone rang.

"Williams here, sir, I thought you'd still be there."

"Are you going to tell me that the prints of Pratt and Dent are on record – but under different names."

"Blimey, sir, that's amazing. How on earth did you know it was those two out of the three?"

"I'll explain when I next see you. Just make a note of each man's details – offences and dates, last known addresses, known associates, and so on.

"Time you've done that, it'll be too late to do anything else tonight. Get off home, and I'll see you here at eight in the morning.

****

Bryce found Williams waiting in his office, and waved him to a chair.

"Right, I'll start," he said.

First, as you said yesterday, for my theory to be viable, it would almost certainly mean someone's ID would be fake. If you're going to have a fake ID, then it's not just the name that needs to be false – the address must be too.

The A to Z shows that the address on Peters'

card exists, but those on Dent's and Pratt's did not. I double-checked with a black cab driver, just in case.

"Actually, we were lucky on two counts. First, I nearly stopped when finding the first fake street, but carried on and found the other.

"Secondly, these villains made a stupid mistake. They should have used a real address on their fake IDs – or at the very least a non-existent number in a real street. I'd have been unlikely to spot that.

"Going back to your point about why the murder didn't happen in Bow. After you left yesterday, I spoke to Mrs Unwin. I asked her to think back to when the bus was drawing up to the Bow Church stop, and to describe everything that she could remember about the scene.

"She thought I was trying to get her to identify the other men standing at the stop with Gates. I wasn't. I wanted her to expand her viewpoint and look back in her memory to beyond the bus stop.

"She mentioned a couple of other things, and then, without any prompting, said that there were two bobbies a few yards past the bus stop. They were walking along on the same side of the road as the bus, but in the opposite direction. She reckoned they hadn't quite drawn parallel with the bus when it moved off.

"To save time, when I rang Mrs Norlake I asked if she had seen a policeman. She immediately corrected me and corroborated what Mrs Unwin had said – she'd also seen two.

"Obviously, the murder couldn't be safely committed at the roadside under the eye of two constables, and so Gates was able to get on the bus.

"Your turn, Williams. Tell me what you've gleaned at the Yard."

"I have to hand it to you about what happened at Bow sir; that certainly gets around my objections.

"Anyway, when the Yard boys got the photographs done, someone must have informed Chief Superintendent Cherrill, because he came out of his office and took a great interest in the cross-checking with the records. Supervised the whole thing himself. He asked me to give him the background, and I can tell you that he was very complimentary about you chasing down what didn't seem a very promising theory!"

"The prints on the statements of Dent and Pratt matched the records of two brothers, Ben and Oscar Daynes. Twins, but not identical. Both nasty bits of business, sir. Each went through the courts several times in the late nineteen twenties and through the thirties. Apart from Ben having one dishonesty charge as a juvenile, all their offences were violent.

"Either separately or together, they both served sentences for common assault, and it seems they acted as enforcers for other criminals. In 1939 they were sentenced to seven years each for grievous bodily harm, so they were in Pentonville all through the war. Released a few months ago, and that's when they decided to change their identities. Top quality forgeries, though.

"Oh, and there were no known prints on the box."

"Excellent," said Bryce. "Now we just have to hope that they are still at – or at least have connections to – their last-known addresses. Where did they live? I hope we're not going to find that the places have been bombed and aren't standing anymore."

"No problem there, sir. Neither brother was married, and they shared a house in Cable Street. Unusually for the area, in 1939 they were owner-occupiers, so I thought there must be a chance they're still there.

"I found Constable Sawyer just before you arrived, sir. He's the beat officer for most of Cable Street. Says there was a lot of bomb damage in the street. One of the bits left standing is the block with the Daynes' house, which survived unscathed. I showed him mugshots and he said immediately they're still living at that address."

"Well done, Sergeant. We can't do much more until we get the two of them in custody. Question is, when's the best time to find them at home?

"Six a.m. is usually a good time."

"Agreed. Let's do that. I'll go and find a

magistrate, and ask for a warrant.

"You arrange for half a dozen officers to meet us here at a quarter to six tomorrow morning. We'll use our two detective constables for a start. See Inspector Collins and ask if we can borrow four of his uniformed men as well. Sawyer might be useful, if he's available as one of the four. Don't tell anyone what the target address is – find Sawyer again now, if you can, and tell him not a word about this to anyone else."

"Very good, sir. Will you be armed?"

"You didn't mention any firearms in the brothers' history, so no, I think not."

****

At five forty-five the next morning, eight police officers assembled in the police station foyer. Bryce explained where they were going, and who they wanted to find, and invited questions and comments.

One of the older uniformed constables chipped in with his experience of the brothers:

"I remember the Daynes twins before the war. Bottom-of-the-barrel dregs, the both of them. They leaned on people for bigger crooks who didn't want to get their hands dirty."

"Seems they're still in the same line of business," said Bryce.

"Oscar, the smaller one, has the brains, sir, and the guts," continued the constable. "I think Ben would be a coward if Oscar wasn't there to think for him and tell him what to do and say."

Bryce thanked the officer, and stepped back to allow Williams to instruct the men on their positions and actions.

Constable Sawyer and another were detailed to cover the back of the property. Everyone else would arrive at the front by car from opposite directions. Two officers would carry the heavy ram used for smashing down doors.

"By the way," Bryce added, "assuming we find them, I propose to arrest them both on suspicion of murder. No fiddling about possessing fake IDs as a holding charge.

"And from the moment we get in, they're to be kept completely separate. I don't want any collusion – no talking, shouting, or silent signals between them. No communication at all. We'll bring them back in different cars, one to Leman Street and the other to Commercial Street. I don't want them to so much as see each other. All understood?"

"Right. Off we go!"

****

Half an hour later, the raid was over. The police had been so quick that neither brother had even managed to leave his bedroom before being pounced on.

They were now sitting in separate police stations, and wondering where they had gone wrong.

Bryce, reflecting on the comment of the officer who had said that Ben, the larger and more brutal-looking brother, was mentally the weaker of the two, decided that he was the best prospect to try and break first under well-applied pressure.

He had arranged for Ben Daynes to be brought into an interview room at Commercial Street, and now he and Williams sat facing the larger twin. The table between them was completely bare. The DI had no need of notes.

"Dear oh dearie me, Ben," Bryce began pleasantly, "you're really in trouble this time. It's back to Pentonville for you. You'll be pleased to learn that you won't have to share a cell, though.

"You won't be kept as long as last time, either. Three clear Sundays after you get in, and then it's the drop for you, followed by burial in the yard."

Daynes was already shaking with fear.

"No guv, it wasn't me," he managed to get out. "It was Oscar what knifed him, honest."

"Honest you certainly are not," retorted Bryce. "But let's see if you can sing us a song that we like. Caution him, Sergeant."

The caution administered, Bryce leaned forward and again spoke pleasantly but more menacingly:

"Off you go then, Ben – verse one. And make sure you hit every note sweet and clear for me; because you've got me out of bed far too early this morning, and I'm in no mood to be messed with!

You two weren't after Gerry Gates on your own account. Who were you working for, Ben?"

"Noddy Springett," replied Daynes without hesitating and still quaking.

"Why – what had Gates done to him?"

"I don't rightly know, guv, an' tha's honest. Me, I never spoke to Noddy about this meself. Oscar said we was just to take Gates out.

"I s'pose he must have messed with Noddy somehow, and people had to be shown you couldn't do that. We did jobs like that for him before the war – you know, just softening people up, like, makin' them more agreeable for Noddy."

"What happened at Bow Church?"

"We was meant to introduce ourselves nicely to Gates, cos he didn't know us, and then persuade him to come with us into the churchyard. Oscar would do the job there.

"But by the bus stop there was two rozzers coming along. So we couldn't make the move, and the bus come before they were clear away. Anyways, he gets on the bus after some other geezer, an' we followed.

"We go up the stairs, Oscar first. At the top, Gates sat hisself in the back seat. Oscar goes and sits next to 'im. I goes and sits in the seat in front of 'em.

"Well, he's immediately twitchy and suspicious, o' course. The bus is almost empty and we're tight up against 'im. So Oscar does the job there and then – quick like. Tells me later that as soon as he saw everyone sitting up front and looking forwards, and me blocking their view if they did turn round, he took his chance.

"I didn't know it then, but Oscar hid the knife in Gates' sleeve. He went and sat nearer the front, an' beckoned me to move up too.

"Neither of us 'ad bin on this bus wiv doors before. I think maybe Oscar forgot for a second that we can't 'op off. Anyway, Oscar decides to stay on board and hope nobody'd notice Gates. He said he meant for us to get off at Aldgate along with everyone else, and thought that Gates wouldn't be found until we were well clear.

"But that woman gets up to get off ages before the stop, sees some blood, so she starts screamin' 'er stoopid 'ead off."

"Tell us about the fake ID cards, Ben."

"While we were still in the 'Ville, Oscar said we needed to lose our old lives and move on as new people. He found some contacts, and when we got out he went to see this geezer in Peckham. Comes back wiv two new cards – well, no, you've seen 'em guv, they was like well-used cards. Don't know how much they cost, but I s'pose Noddy or someone else paid. But I didn't go to Peckham, and I don't know who the geezer is, or his address. Honest."

"I wish you wouldn't keep using that word, Ben," said Bryce, "it pains me to hear it from your criminal lips."

"Anyway, would you like to make a

statement now?"

"Yes I would guv. I'm not going to swing for this. I'll turn King's Evidence."

"Not up to me whether you can do that, Ben. Do you want a lawyer before we start?"

"No, I don't hold with lawyers." (Williams, who had only discovered yesterday that his boss was a lawyer, smiled inwardly at the irony of this situation.)

"Do you want to write your statement on your own, or would you like us to help?"

"I can read good, and I can write fair, but I wouldn't know what to put."

"Okay," said the DI, I'll suggest things to say. If you agree, just write it down. If you don't agree, make sure you say so.

"Start off like this:

"My name is Benjamin Daynes, also known as Alan Dent."

Bryce went on, giving Daynes time to write each short sentence in his laboured fashion. The statement continued:

"I live at 450 Cable Street. I want to make a statement. I have been told I can have a solicitor present, but I choose not to have one."

It took an hour to complete the statement. It included phrases about not being offered inducements or promises of any kind, and – at the end – that the author had read everything and had been invited to alter anything before signing.

Bryce told Daynes to read it again very

carefully, and then to sign it if he was happy.

That done, Bryce told Daynes he should still consider getting a solicitor – but not one that his brother might be using. The DI also said that he'd arrange to get him a cup of tea and a good breakfast, and the man was taken back to the cells.

"Well done, sir, that's Oscar all tied up nicely," said Williams, who hadn't said a word during the interview. "A masterclass, I think they call it, on how to get a man to dob someone else in."

"I can't say I feel particularly sorry for Ben, even though he's evidently completely under his brother's thumb," said Bryce. "He'll probably hang too."

"How's that, sir?"

"The two men were involved in a joint enterprise – they both went out with the intention to kill. Ben is equally guilty in law.

"Before your time, of course – it's nearly twenty years ago – but you'll have heard of Browne and Kennedy, involved in the murder of a police officer. Only Browne fired the shots, and Kennedy expected to be charged with something less than murder. But his own evidence actually helped hang both of them. This may be the same.

"Yes, Ben's helped the police. But we can produce quite a bit of evidence against both brothers. With Ben's statement, there should be enough to convict both of them. The Prosecution may agree to allow Ben to turn King's Evidence, but I don't think it'll be necessary.

"Even if they do, and Ben gets off with a lesser sentence, he's finished. Everyone in his circle will know he's sent his own brother to the gallows.

"Let's go and get ourselves some breakfast before we see Oscar at Leman Street."

****

Oscar Daynes was a shorter and flimsier version of his brother. For all his shifty looks, there were nevertheless signs of intelligence that his twin lacked. There was also an arrogance about Oscar which Bryce hoped to see eliminated by the time he had finished with him.

Sitting down opposite the detectives, Daynes immediately opened up with:

"You're wastin' your time, Mr Bryce."

"Maybe, maybe not," said Bryce. "We'll see. Either way, it's my time and I've got plenty of it. Remains to be seen if you've got plenty of time left yourself, though, Oscar."

There was a grim hardness to Bryce's words and manner. He continued:

"I've arrested you on suspicion of murder, Daynes. Sergeant Williams will caution you now."

The caution administered, Bryce asked:

"Would you like a solicitor?"

"No point. I've done nuffink, and I'm sayin' nuffink."

"As you wish. I'm going to put various questions to you, and your replies – or your silence

– will be noted.

"Where did you get your fake ID card?"

"Who says it's fake?"

"I do, for a start, Oscar. Your dabs say you're Oscar Daynes, with a long record. Your ID says you're Paul Pratt. Have you changed you name officially, by deed poll, for example?"

"It's not illegal to call yourself what you like."

"Quite true, Oscar – as long as you don't do it to defraud. But at present it's also illegal to use a false ID card." Bryce paused and looked at Williams sitting beside him:

"Do you know any good identity card forgers, Sergeant?"

Williams was commendably quick on the uptake.

"I've heard there's a crackingly good one in Peckham, sir. Take me no time whatsoever to have him pulled in for you right now," said the Sergeant, adding extra force to his pretence that he knew the forger's address by rising from his chair.

"We'll do that next, Sergeant, after we've finished here. Don't suppose your low-life in Peckham would want to be involved in murder, would he, Oscar?"

This exchange was a palpable hit; Daynes couldn't help showing surprise at the mention of Peckham, and was silent. Bryce moved on.

"Let's talk about when you were outside Bow Church. You saw the two policemen coming along, so you decided to follow Gates onto the bus, rather than do the job there – or better still – under the trees in the churchyard."

"Who's Gates?" asked Daynes.

"Oh, you know Gerry Gates, Oscar – he's the man Noddy told you to silence."

Again, Daynes was taken aback. Struggling to keep his voice and expression unconcerned, he tried to think what else the DI might know and what he should say next.

"Don't know no Noddy," he offered lamely.

"Really. Well, Mr Springett's coming in too – we'll see what he has to say.

"He knows already that you bungled the job. And that you left the box of diamonds on the body instead of grabbing it and taking it back. I doubt he's a happy man at the moment

"In fact, if we hadn't got you safely in here, Oscar, I guess he'd be looking for a more efficient catspaw, to show everyone that he doesn't tolerate incompetence in his henchmen.

"I was going to offer you some breakfast, but perhaps you'd better get someone to taste your food – in case his reach extends even into the nick!"

Daynes looked very unhappy indeed. He sat motionless and silent. Eventually, he looked up and said:

"I want a mouthpiece."

"Good idea," said Bryce. "Anyone in particular?"

"I want to make a 'phone call, and I don't

want nobody listenin'."

"Agreed. Sergeant, take him up to my office. The telephone in there is an outside line.

"Oscar, Sergeant Williams will wait outside until you've finished, and I promise you that he won't be able to hear."

Bryce remained where he was until Williams returned about ten minutes later.

"I've put him back in the cell, sir. He made his call, and then said he wasn't saying anything more until his lawyer arrives. Within an hour, he says."

"Good. Get on to the exchange right away and find out the number or numbers he called. Then check who those numbers belong to. If he's as dim as his brother, he might just have called this Noddy to ask for his help. I'll bet he doesn't have a solicitor himself.

"When you've done that, find out where this Springett man lives. I've heard the name, but can't place him. The Yard can probably help. If you find an address, take a DC and pick him up. If he doesn't want to attend the station voluntarily, arrest him on suspicion of conspiracy to commit murder.

"Okay, sir. If you don't mind my asking – why didn't you tell Oscar that his brother had already squealed?"

"Gut feeling, really. I've dropped a couple of hints, of course – letting him know about Peckham and about Noddy. But we might have picked those bits up from other sources. I just thought it'd be better to hold back for the moment the fact that his brother's grassed him up."

****

Bryce returned to his office to do some more of his court paperwork.

In no time at all Williams stuck his head round the door to report first that the number Daynes had called was indeed Springett's, and second that he had an address for the man, and was on his way.

"Out in Camberwell, sir, quite posh. They know of him at the local nick."

"Okay. Call at the station first. Might be politically sound to ask if one of the 'P' Division boys would like to accompany you."

Williams left and Bryce returned to his paperwork, until half an hour later the desk sergeant called to say that Daynes' solicitor had arrived. The DI told him to put the man in an interview room, and he would come down immediately.

The solicitor was on the right side of thirty, clean-shaven and very smartly dressed. Extending a hand, he introduced himself as Walter Percival.

"You are holding my client, Oscar Daynes. On what charge?"

"Suspicion of murder. He's been formally cautioned. As yet he hasn't been charged."

"I'd like to see him."

"Of course, Mr Percival. If you wait here a

moment, I'll have him brought into this interview room immediately. Unless you advise him to remain silent, perhaps you'll let me know when he is ready to be questioned further."

The DI found the desk sergeant and told him to have Percival taken to the interview room.

Deciding a cup of coffee would be welcome, Bryce took himself off to the staff canteen and whiled away twenty minutes, judging this to be sufficient time for Daynes and his representative to have a chat.

Back in the interview room, the solicitor wasted no time in making demands before the DI had even shut the door:

"I understand you are also holding Mr Ben Daynes here, Inspector. Before Mr Oscar Daynes says anything further, I want to see Ben."

"I don't think so."

"I do think so!" parodied the solicitor with a supercilious smile, "I have the right to see him."

Daynes brightened considerably as he watched this terse exchange. One-nil to his mouthpiece, he thought, and looked forward to more of the same.

"You have no such right, Mr Percival. And don't presume to lecture me on the law – I'm a barrister. You have no right to see him because he has already made a statement specifically saying – in his own handwriting – that he doesn't hold with lawyers and doesn't want one. At present you have no standing.

"If he changes his mind – and I've suggested that he should – then of course he can have the solicitor of his choice. He is being held at a different police station, incidentally.

"I've also mentioned that in my opinion he would certainly be better served by appointing someone who isn't also representing his brother.

"You see, in his statement, which incidentally is very detailed, he says that your client here was paid to murder Gerry Gates. And he explains exactly how that was done.

"He wants to turn King's Evidence. I've told him that I can promise nothing, and in his statement he confirms that he understands that. I don't know how the Crown will play this one. But if they don't allow him that route, the alternative looks like being the 'cutthroat defence', Either way, I'm sure you agree that separate representation at trial will be essential."

Daynes had been growling and muttering ever since Bryce dropped the bombshell about what Ben had said. His earlier confidence had evaporated. Now he started tapping his head and furiously exclaimed:

"You don't want to believe anything Ben says; he's not all there."

Percival told him to remain silent. The solicitor thought for a moment.

"I'd like to see the statement of Ben Daynes."

"I'm sure you would. But you're not seeing it. I'm still gathering evidence. I haven't even charged

Ben Daynes yet, although I have ample grounds.

"When I decide to charge your client, that'll be time enough for you to see the evidence against him. Which, incidentally, will hang him.

"Oh, and by the way, Mr Percival. No doubt Noddy Springett is paying for you to represent Oscar here. So I guess he is also a more regular client of yours. It might be worth your while hanging around for a bit – we're bringing Springett in as soon as we can find him.

"Actually, I suppose there might be a further conflict of interest there. But that's up to you."

There was a short silence. At length, Percival said:

"I don't deny that Mr Springett is a regular client, and if there is a conflict – and I'm not saying there is – I think he must take priority."

"You mean you'll leave me in the lurch!" shouted Daynes, angrily.

"No, no, my dear chap. It's just that we might have to find a different solicitor for you.

"I'll have another chat with Mr Daynes, Inspector. It may be that he'll maintain his right to remain silent. Or he may decide to make a statement. Or he may decide to appoint a different lawyer."

"Fair enough, Mr Percival," said Bryce, his tone at its most pleasant as he prepared to deliver yet another broadside to the criminal and his adviser.

"There's something else your client might

want your help with before you leave. He told us under caution in his earlier interview that he didn't know Mr Springett.

"Perhaps he'd like to explain why his one telephone call earlier was to that gentleman – and how he had the man's number in his head."

Daynes immediately started ranting about being promised that nobody would listen. Every other word he spat out was a curse word.

"Nobody listened, Oscar," replied Bryce, calmly, "although actually a call to your employer wasn't privileged, like a call to your solicitor would have been. In fact, all we did was ask the exchange which number you called."

Bryce left them to it, telling the constable on guard outside the door to stay alert in case the prisoner made a run for it.

****

At one o'clock Bryce went out for something to eat. On his return, he learned from the desk sergeant that Williams had returned with Donald Springett.

"Something else you should know, sir. Apparently that solicitor told Daynes that he couldn't represent him, and there was a rare old ding-dong in the interview after you left. Constable Edgar had to get help to take Daynes back to the cells."

Williams appeared as they were speaking.

"Springett's attending voluntarily, sir. I've

got him in the interview room. Cool as a cucumber. There was a solicitor here, a man named Percival – I understand you saw him earlier – and he said he represented Springett. But Springett said he would deal with this himself and sent him away."

"I wonder if Springett has heard of the old adage: 'a man who represents himself has a fool for a client'," said Bryce.

Both officers laughed. Williams added:

"Before he left, Percival asked me to tell you that he couldn't represent Oscar Daynes after all. Strange man – very well dressed but looked as though he'd been in a brawl. He'll have a right shiner on his left eye tomorrow."

The desk sergeant guffawed, and explained.

Bryce gave Williams the gist of the latest developments:

"Before we talk to Springett, I should tell you that I spoke to Percival in Oscar's presence, and told him about Ben's statement. He wanted to see Ben, but I refused. I also refused to let him see Ben's statement.

"Percival appreciated that he can't represent both brothers under the circumstances. Then, when I told him Springett was coming in, he admitted that he is a regular client and loyalty to him means – in the event of a conflict of interest there as well – that he would have to ditch Oscar. It would seem that Percival has now accepted that he can't represent both, which is actually quite telling in itself."

To the desk sergeant, Bryce said:

"Gates, get someone to bring us a jug of decent coffee, please, with a separate milk jug and a sugar bowl, and three cups. Come on Williams, let's go and see him."

In the interview room they found a man of about fifty, short and corpulent. He had a fringe of greying hair around an otherwise bald head and wore spectacles with very thick lenses. He looked nothing at all like a hardened criminal, and could easily have passed for a professor in any university corridor.

Bryce introduced himself and his colleague, and – to Williams' surprise – shook hands.

"Take a seat, Mr Springett. We have a very serious matter to discuss with you. I understand that you have seen your solicitor, but have decided to carry on without him. I'm not sure how much he has told you, but I'll detail everything anyway.

"First, I'll emphasise that you aren't under arrest, but I think it is only fair that you are interviewed under caution. Sergeant, if you please...

"I won't beat about the bush. We have the two Daynes brothers in custody. They have both been arrested on suspicion of the murder of Gerry Gates, who is a jeweller of some sort.

"Daynes says that Gates was killed on your instructions. What do you say to that?

"Quite ludicrous, Inspector," came the modulated tones of the mobster. "I have no idea who these people are. I don't know anyone of the name of Daynes. I'm rather distressed, in fact, to have been brought here, although I came voluntarily when asked."

"I see," said Bryce. "Well perhaps you know Alan Dent and Paul Pratt?"

Springett hesitated briefly and Bryce surmised that he didn't want to deny something that might be easily provable.

"Yes, I know them very slightly. They sometimes do small jobs for me."

"I'm sure they do, Mr Springett. And possibly some bigger jobs, too?"

Springett didn't bat an eyelid at the suggestion.

A constable came in with the coffee and Bryce poured, pushing cups towards Williams and Springett.

"Help yourselves to milk and sugar."

When Springett was done stirring, Bryce resumed his questioning:

"What about poor dead Gerry Gates?"

"I don't think I've ever heard of him, Inspector."

"Well, just take a look at this. It's a picture of the late, unfortunate Gates." He pulled a rolled-up photograph from his pocket and handed it to Springett, who unrolled and examined it before handing it back.

"Not a pretty sight, Inspector, but it still rings no bells."

"I see. What's your line of work, Mr Springett?"

"Oh, I buy and sell things, antiques, other bits and pieces."

"What about diamonds – uncut diamonds, in particular?"

"Certainly not, inspector. I know nothing about things like that. Highly specialised, diamonds are."

"Hmm. Look, Mr Springett, I haven't quite finished, but I've just realised the Sergeant and I need to do something. Wait here for five minutes, please."

Outside, Bryce said to Williams:

"Get his prints off this photograph, and compare those with the ones you took of the inside and outside of the box. I wasn't sure if he'd hold the photograph, so we've got the coffee cup and milk jug to fall back on. If you can't lift anything from this, we'll try those. As soon as you've taken a look, come back in and give me an unobtrusive nod if there's a match – or a shake of the head if there isn't."

Bryce went down to the cells to see Oscar Daynes, who was now looking very downcast.

"Just one question, Oscar. We've established that you did know Springett. When did you first do any work of any sort for him?"

"I dunno. About 1937, I should think. Why?"

Bryce didn't deign to answer, but told the custody officer to lock the cell again.

He returned to the interview room, and apologised to Springett for the delay.

"You denied knowing the real names of the men now known as Dent and Pratt. So you didn't know that they both have extensive criminal records?

"Certainly not, Inspector. Horrified to hear you say so."

"When did you first employ them on your, jobs?"

"I don't remember exactly. Quite recently. A few months ago."

"So you had no inkling that they'd had both just been released after each serving seven years for a serious assault?"

"No – Again, Inspector, I'm deeply shocked to learn it. I'd never have employed criminals."

"Tell me more about the work that you gave these two. What sort of jobs?"

"Oh, arranging transport for various items from A to B, carrying urgent messages, that sort of thing"

"Why did it need two of them to 'carry a message'?"

"It didn't always. Sometimes I only used one."

There was a tap on the door, and Williams came in again. He nodded to Bryce as he sat down.

"Let's go over a couple of things again. Mr Springett. You say you would never employ jailbirds. And you know nothing about diamonds.

"It's very strange then, is it not, that both Dent and Pratt state that they worked for you before the war – long before either of them acquired their new monikers?"

Springett was silent for a moment, and then said:

"Their word against mine, Inspector. And I'm a man of good character, whereas from what you tell me they are seasoned criminals."

"Well, if it ever comes to a difference of opinion in a courtroom Mr Springett, it'll be for the jury to decide who is telling the truth.

"But let's move on to the matter of the diamonds. As you don't know Gerry Gates, you obviously won't know that he was carrying a special case, chained to his wrist. In the case were rough diamonds.

"How do you explain that your fingerprints appear both inside and outside that case?"

Finally, Springett looked concerned, and gave no answer. Eventually he said, with an attempt at a smile:

"You took my dabs off that photograph, I suppose?"

"Correct. But your coffee cup there would have been the back-up."

"Donald Springett, I'm arresting you on suspicion of murder. Would you like to make a statement? Or would you prefer to see Mr Percival after all?"

"Get me Percival," said Springett through

clenched teeth.

Bryce beckoned Williams outside. Once out of earshot, the DI said:

"Take someone with you, and get him down to Limehouse immediately, and booked in there. I don't want him going near the cells here or in Commercial Street. I want to eliminate any chance of the three of them communicating with each other. We'll charge all three of them later today – just let them sweat a bit first.

"Another masterclass for me to witness, sir; this time on how to get someone to incriminate himself. Congratulations. And you were right about that 'fool for a client' saying.

"There must be enough to convict, now."

"I'm confident, yes. But I expect Springett to change his story, and claim he only intended the brothers to give Gates a beating – as they had obviously done on his instructions before. That will reinforce the case against the brothers, but it won't save him, though."

****

AFTERWORD

Historical note on the bus appearing in this story.

For many years, buses (and trams and trolley buses) in London had been operated with a driver and a conductor. The conductor roamed around the bus, on both decks in the case of double-deckers. He or she collected fares and issued receipts ('tickets'). Entry to most double-decker buses was via an open platform, and people could – and did – get on or off while the vehicle was moving reasonably slowly.

In 1945, just after the end of WW2, the London Transport Passenger Board ('London Transport') started experimenting with 'Pay As You Board' arrangements. However, at the time there seems to have been no suggestion of making economies by abolishing the conductor and having driver-only buses – as is the norm almost everywhere today.

Instead, the conductor became a stationary, rather than roving, figure. A seat was provided for him just inside the entrance.

Initially, two 1934 STL buses (both models with front entrance doors) and a 1933 X1 trolley bus (centre doors) were modified to allow a seated conductor.

A little later, a bomb-damaged RT bus – RT97, the vehicle in this story – was added to the little experimental fleet. This, like all RTs, originally had an open low-level rear platform. Doors were fitted to the (now raised) platform, and a rear-facing seat provided for the conductor.

There were other changes – for example additional emergency exits were provided, and the staircase was moved. The modifications resulted in 6 fewer seats downstairs, so that the total seating capacity became 50. (There remained room for standing passengers too, of course, but probably slightly fewer than before).

On the busy Kingston route with close-set stops to which it was allocated, it was unsuccessful. Passengers had to congregate on the platform while earlier arrivals paid their fares. This often held up the bus. Passengers disliked this, being used to boarding a bus and generally being able to sit down at once, after which the conductor would come to them. The change was particularly difficult for elderly or disabled passengers, of course, who found standing on what effectively became a waiting area was problematic once the bus started moving. The modified vehicles were never popular.

One can only wonder at the idea behind this experiment. By any measurement, it seems to have been a failure.

It isn't clear from where LT expected cost savings to materialise. The 12% reduction in seating capacity alone would mean that the cost-benefit was hampered from the outset. The cost of modification, and the cost of delays en route, must have resulted in an entirely foreseeable negative benefit. And that is before taking into account the dissatisfaction of the paying customers!

RT97 only lasted on service 65 for three months. LT seems to have decided that PAYB on a Green Line route with longer distances between stops might be more fruitful. So, the bus was transferred to the 721 service between Aldgate and Romford (which is where it was running in this story).

It was no more successful in its new green livery. Barely four months later, in July 1946, the PAYB experiment was abandoned and RT97 was once again given a roving conductor.

This bus had a uniquely chequered history. Introduced as an ordinary red bus in 1940, it had been badly bomb-damaged in 1944, and then in 1946 converted first into a red PAYB, then into a green PAYB, and then into a regular bus again.

That wasn't the end of its career. For its last eight or so years with LT, it was used for other experiments – engine arrangements, passenger heating, fluorescent lighting, window design, etc. By that time it can have borne little resemblance to its original form, although as far as is known its 9.6 litre 6-cylinder diesel engine remained to the end.

LT sold it in 1955, and it was used by a football pools company in Liverpool as a staff bus. It was eventually scrapped in 1961.

BOOKS BY THIS AUTHOR

The Bedroom Window Murder

It is 1949. Sir Francis Sherwood – WW1 hero, landowner, magistrate – is shot dead while standing at an open bedroom window in his country house. A rifle is found in the grounds.

The county police seek help from Scotland Yard. Detective Chief Inspector Bryce and Detective Sergeant Haig are assigned to the case. The first difficulty for the Yard men is that nobody with even a mild dislike of Sherwood can be found. But before that problem can be resolved, others arise......

The Courthouse Murder

In July 1949, an unpopular and deeply unpleasant man is stabbed in the courthouse of an English city. As the murder has been committed in a room to which the general public doesn't have access, it seems probable that the culprit is someone involved with the business of the courts.

Suspects include a number of lawyers, police officers, and magistrates.

For various reasons, the local Chief Constable decides to ask Scotland Yard to investigate the murder. Chief Inspector Philip Bryce and Sergeant Alex Haig are assigned to the case.

Theirs is a recent partnership, but the two men worked well together in another murder case a few weeks before. (See 'The Bedroom Window Murder'.)

The Felixstowe Murder

In August 1949, Detective Chief Inspector Bryce and his new bride Veronica are holidaying in the East Anglian resort of Felixstowe.

During afternoon tea in the Palm Court of their hotel, a man dies at a nearby table.

Reluctant to get directly involved, Bryce nevertheless agrees to help the inexperienced local police inspector get to grips with his first murder case, turning his honeymoon into a 'busman's holiday'.

Printed in Great Britain
by Amazon